KU-736-991

# *Summer Brides*

*Two unexpected journeys to 'I do'—
two perfect summer weddings…*

Stunning Ashley Marsh and beautiful doctor
Charlotte Johnson have vowed never to risk
it all for love—but the hotshot docs they
work with are an irresistible temptation!

ER doc Kiefer Bradford and army doc
Jackson Hilstead are hotter than the summer
sun, and before they know it these two
guarded heroines find their vows undone…

Now they must find the courage
to make the most important vows of all.
And what could be more romantic than
not one but *two* summer weddings?

Find out what happens in:

*White Wedding for a Southern Belle*
by Susan Carlisle

*Wedding Date with the Army Doc*
by Lynne Marshall

**Summer Brides**

Available now!

Dear Reader

I've had a love affair with Savannah, Georgia, for over thirty years. I should—I spent my honeymoon there! The setting of this book made it extra-fun to write. When my fabulous fellow Medical author Lynne Marshall suggested that we place our Summer Brides books in Savannah I didn't hesitate to agree.

I knew who my characters would be as well. Ashley, a feisty local politician who believes deeply in improving her community, and Kiefer, a doctor who starts a clinic in the neighbourhood. These two have so much in common, but both have such strong personalities they almost can't get past themselves to see the love they have for the other.

It was an exciting story to write, and I hope you enjoy reading it. I love to hear from my readers. You can find me at SusanCarlisle.com.

*Susan*

# WHITE WEDDING FOR A SOUTHERN BELLE

BY
SUSAN CARLISLE

STIRLING
COUNCIL
LIBRARIES

MILLS &
BOON

HarperCollins
PUBLISHERS
Since 1817

All rights reserved including the right of reproduction in whole or in part in any form. This edition is published by arrangement with Harlequin Books S.A.

This is a work of fiction. Names, characters, places, locations and incidents are purely fictional and bear no relationship to any real life individuals, living or dead, or to any actual places, business establishments, locations, events or incidents. Any resemblance is entirely coincidental.

This book is sold subject to the condition that it shall not, by way of trade or otherwise, be lent, resold, hired out or otherwise circulated without the prior consent of the publisher in any form of binding or cover other than that in which it is published and without a similar condition including this condition being imposed on the subsequent purchaser.

® and TM are trademarks owned and used by the trademark owner and/or its licensee. Trademarks marked with ® are registered with the United Kingdom Patent Office and/or the Office for Harmonisation in the Internal Market and in other countries.

First published in Great Britain 2016
By Mills & Boon, an imprint of HarperCollins*Publishers*
1 London Bridge Street, London, SE1 9GF

Large Print edition 2017

© 2016 Susan Carlisle

ISBN: 978-0-263-06673-9

Our policy is to use papers that are natural, renewable and recyclable products and made from wood grown in sustainable forests. The logging and manufacturing processes conform to the legal environmental regulations of the country of origin.

Printed and bound in Great Britain
by CPI Antony Rowe, Chippenham, Wiltshire

**Susan Carlisle**'s love affair with books began in the sixth grade, when she made a bad grade in maths. Not allowed to watch TV until she brought the grade up, Susan filled her time with books. She turned her love of reading into a passion for writing, and now has over ten Medical Romances published through Mills & Boon. She writes about hot, sexy docs and the strong women who captivate them. Visit SusanCarlisle.com.

### Books by Susan Carlisle

### Mills & Boon Medical Romance

#### *Midwives On-Call*
*His Best Friend's Baby*

#### *Heart of Mississippi*
*The Maverick Who Ruled Her Heart*
*The Doctor Who Made Her Love Again*

*Snowbound with Dr Delectable*
*The Rebel Doc Who Stole Her Heart*
*The Doctor's Redemption*
*One Night Before Christmas*
*Married for the Boss's Baby*

Visit the Author Profile page at millsandboon.co.uk for more titles.

To Joan May, my mother-in-law.
Thanks for sharing your son with me.

**Praise for
Susan Carlisle**

'Gripping, stirring, and emotionally touching…
A perfect Medical read!'

—*Goodreads* on
*His Best Friend's Baby*

'This emotional love story kept me riveted. A
truly satisfying, emotional read. Susan Carlisle's
work is like that. Check it out, you won't be
disappointed.'

—*Goodreads* on
*NYC Angels: The Wallflower's Secret*

# CHAPTER ONE

ASHLEY MARSH PUSHED through the crowded ball-room filled with St. Patrick's Day revelers dressed in costumes and lit by nothing but small green lights. As an alderman on the Savannah City Council, part of her job was to attend these types of events. Still, a fund-raiser hosted by Maggie Bradford wasn't an invitation she could ignore.

Savannah, Georgia, with its large Irish history and a disposition toward a good party did St. Paddy's Day right, even to the point of turning the river green. She'd always enjoyed the festivities but costume parties were a little over the top for her. Recognizing who she was speaking to tonight probably wasn't going to happen. It made her a little nervous knowing that when people were behind a mask they tended to do things they wouldn't otherwise. Experience told her that she wasn't always a good judge of character anyway.

The crowd around her wore anything from big

green shamrock glasses to Irish kilts. She'd chosen a green tunic and tights, and a leprechaun hat. With a glittery gold mask over her eyes, she had some anonymity yet she didn't look as foolish as many of those in the room. She smiled to herself. More than once someone had told her to lighten up. Maybe tonight she would…a little. After all, few in the room could identify her.

"Ms. Marsh."

Maybe she was wrong.

She knew that voice. It was Alderman Henderson, a thorn in her side most of the time. He was dressed as if he were the mayor of an Irish village in a green suit with yellow plaid vest and buckled top hat.

"Ralph, how're you doing? Having a good time?" She already knew he wasn't.

He shrugged. "I guess so. The wife is really into these things. Anyway, I want to let you know that the hospital has agreed to partner with us on your clinic idea. I just spoke to the administrator a few minutes ago. I'm going to agree to support it for the trial period of six months. Be aware, if there's just one issue I'm going to withdraw that support." His tone was firm, indicating he wouldn't be changing his mind if all didn't go well with the clinic.

Excitement filled her. She'd been working for this opportunity since she'd been elected. "Thanks, Ralph. You're doing the right thing here."

"I'm not sure about that yet, so we'll see." He wandered off into the crowd and Ashley wasn't disappointed.

Suddenly feeling like celebrating, she looked around the room and spied a tall man with brown hair standing by himself. He was near a door to the outside as if he was preparing to run at any moment. He wore a dark suit with a green tie. Over his eyes was a mask of small yellow plaid. He was certainly understated for the occasion. Surely he would be safe enough for a dance or two?

Ashley made her way in his direction. Stopping in front of him, she said, "Happy St. Patrick's Day. How about giving a leprechaun a bit of luck by dancing with her?"

Dark green eyes looked at her for a long moment. He nodded then set the drink he held down on a nearby table. Following her, they moved out onto the dance floor. A fast song was playing and she turned to face him. The man was a good dancer. They shared two more songs.

When a slow number started she said, "Thank you for the dances."

He inclined his head. "You're welcome." The sexy timbre in his deep, rich voice was something she wouldn't soon forget.

Ashley walked away. She wasn't into being held by strange men, so she was both surprised and relieved that he hadn't insisted she dance the slower song. If she was less cautious she might have enjoyed being in this stranger's arms, but she knew too well what could happen when you weren't careful…

Dr. Kiefer Bradford watched the tiny leprechaun cross the room and speak to a few people as she left him on the dance floor. He might have pursued her but his mother wouldn't appreciate him picking up a one-night stand at her event and he'd no interest in anything longer. After what his ex-wife had done to him he had no intention of stepping into a serious relationship again. She'd seen to it that he didn't believe anything a woman said.

The only reason he was at his mother's costume ball was because he'd been in town for a job interview. When his former best friend, Josh—now his ex-wife's husband—had been made director of the ER at the Atlanta hospital where Kiefer worked, it had been time for him to get out of town.

He was tired of dodging Josh. The whispers of the staff. The pitying faces of his friends. And, worse, the anger he continued to feel. Savannah was his home. He still owned a place here. He'd come back and leave all the ugliness behind.

Kiefer saw the leprechaun a few more times around the room but never on the dance floor. Twice they were almost close enough to speak but then she was gone. Anyway, he'd done his duty and he was ready to go. Enough green for him today. He'd watch and hear the rest of the fun from the balcony of his apartment.

As he was on his way out to the lobby, the leprechaun was coming out of a door to the right. Just as he was about to pass her Kiefer saw his ex-wife, Brittney, and Josh coming toward him among a group of people. Despite the festive dress, he recognized them.

Apprehension and anger rushed through him.

Even here they still interrupted his life. They must have come to town for St. Patrick's Day. Brittney was from Savannah as well. Regardless of their history, his mother's party was the go-to event in town, so of course they wouldn't miss it.

Kiefer didn't want to speak with Brittney and Josh or want them to see him leaving alone. Without thinking, he grabbed the leprechaun as she passed.

Her small yelp of surprise made him pause for a second before his mouth found hers and he backed her against the wall. Her lips were soft and sweet beneath his. Her hands braced against his chest, pushed and then relaxed against him. Seconds later they slid to his waist. He shifted his mouth to gain a better advantage. One of his hands moved to cup her cheek.

Through the fog of desire welling up Kiefer heard the group pass. He forced himself to back away, letting his lips slowly leave the leprechaun's. The longing to find them again filled him but he'd already stepped over the line.

"Just what do you think you're doing?" she hissed, standing between him and the wall, his hand still cupping her face.

"Saying thank you for those dances."

The leprechaun huffed. "By accosting me?"

He shrugged and removed his hand. As he did so the button on the sleeve of his coat caught in the necklace around her neck.

"Stop. Be careful. Don't break it." Her voice rose.

*Why was she overreacting about a simple necklace with a funny-looking stone on it?*

He held his arm motionless while she worked to release the chain. The shamrock on top of her hat bobbed against his nose. She smelled like baking cookies.

"Got it." She looked up.

This leprechaun had the most beautiful doe-brown eyes he'd ever seen. Kiefer leaned in. She pushed against his chest. He stumbled backward and she hurried past him, disappearing into the crowded ballroom.

That leprechaun had certainly made this St. Patrick's Day memorable.

*Three months later*

Kiefer was back in Savannah and driving through Southriver. He wasn't having his first reservation or second but third about being in this part of town at this time of day. During his teen and college years Southriver had been the area where everyone had gone to find or buy a good time. Apparently that hadn't changed.

When the medical director of Savannah Medical Center had questioned him about working at the Southriver clinic during the interview, Kiefer had thought of it as more of a what-if sort of question instead of a sure thing. He liked the adrenaline rush a large ER offered but he needed to get out of Atlanta. Seeing Josh regularly after what he and Brittney had done to him wasn't working. The staff was too aware of the tension between them.

Being the clinic physician wasn't his first choice but at least it would prove his leadership and organizational skills for an opportunity down the road. Three to six months at the clinic and maybe he could transfer to the ER or apply for a departmental spot at the hospital.

As he continued down the street the number of people sitting on the steps of houses increased. It was already hot and steamy for the early days of summer and this evening was no different. These people were doing anything they could to catch a breeze. In front of a few homes children played. Maybe the revitalization of the area was starting to work.

The appearance of the neighborhood improved the farther he drove. The blocks behind him had empty buildings with grass growing in the cracks of the sidewalk and trash blown against the curb. All signs of inner-city apathy. In contrast, the closer he came to the address he was looking for, the better kept the houses and businesses looked. Many were newly painted, with fresh signs above storefronts and flowering plants hung from light posts. This went on for one block but the next started showing the neglected look of the earlier ones.

*What the...?*

Just ahead of him a group of males who wore their pants low on their hips and matching bandannas on their biceps stood aggressively facing a woman in front of a three-story brownstone. The woman was Ashley Marsh. Kiefer recognized her from a couple of TV interviews he'd seen since his return.

The best he could tell, she was a crusader of the highest order. As a child of someone who took on causes—sometimes to her own detriment—he was weary of what Ashley's plans might be. In her interviews he'd found her articulate and intelligent, if not a little antagonistic for his taste.

Kiefer wasn't particularly impressed. He believed in helping people—after all, that was why he'd become a doctor—but he also expected people to help themselves. Not everyone could be saved. Sometimes people were just not worth it.

What he knew of Ashley Marsh reminded Kiefer too much of his mother. That "help everyone, all people are good" view of life made Kiefer a little leery of Ashley Marsh. Advocates often saw the picture through rose-colored glasses. Ms. Marsh struck him as being that type of person. If he were ever interested in a woman again it wouldn't be in someone who didn't show more restraint where people were concerned.

As he drew closer he could see that Ashley was talking to the group, gesturing with her hands.

One of the young men made an aggressive move forward. To her credit, she didn't back away.

Kiefer's hands tightened on the wheel. All the ugly memories of a day so long ago, when his mother had been attacked, came flooding back.

The man off the street, his mother begging him not to kill her, his mother falling to the floor, the man going through her purse and Kiefer watching it all helplessly through the slats of the pantry door. He'd sworn then he would never again stand idly by while someone was being threatened.

His tires squealed as he quickly pulled into a parking lot next to the building. The group turned toward him. At least their attention was drawn away from Alderman Marsh. Kiefer hopped out and circled the truck, putting himself between her and the gang.

"Hey, man, who're you?" growled the man Kiefer had pegged as the leader of the group. His dark hair was long and pulled back in a band. He wore a hoop in his ear.

"Dr. Kiefer Bradford. I'm the new clinic doctor."

"We don't need no more outsiders here."

Ashley sidestepped Kiefer. He put his arm out to stop her without taking his eyes off the men in front of him. He felt more than saw her move around him and he dropped his arm in frustration.

"I can handle this," she announced in a firm tone, confronting the guy in front of Kiefer. "Look, Marko, the clinic is to help the people around here, not to spy on you. What if your mother or sister needed medical care? Don't you want them to have a place to get it? This will be a no-questions-asked place."

*It would be?* That was the first Kiefer had heard of that.

"We don't need…" Marko lifted his chin toward Kiefer "…no outsiders coming into our neighborhood."

"This is my home as much as it is yours," Ashley stated. "I've known your family all your life. I used to change your diapers."

A couple of Marko's buddies snickered. He glanced at them. Their faces sobered. "All your do-gooding isn't going to work," Marko said to Ashley.

"I'm trying to make the community better. The clinic is the first step in doing that."

"Yeah, right, it's your way of trying to change everything." He spit on the ground then scowled. "I run this 'hood, and if I don't want you or your clinic, you'll be gone."

Kiefer took a step forward. "Don't threaten the lady."

Marko glowered at him. "Back off, mister, or you'll regret it."

A couple of Marko's thugs moved toward him.

Ashley pulled at Kiefer's arm, preventing him from going toward Marko. "He isn't worth it."

The horn of a police car had Marko's gang scrambling, each running in a different direction and disappearing into the dwindling light.

"Is there a problem here?" the patrolman asked out the car window.

Ashley left Kiefer's side and went to the car. "No, we're fine, Carl."

Carl looked at Kiefer and raised his chin. "Who's this guy?"

"This is Dr. Bradford, the new director of the clinic."

Kiefer nodded.

"Good to have you, Doc," Carl said. "Never a dull moment in Southriver."

"I'm finding that out."

"Carl, don't run him off before he even gets started," Ashley said with a half laugh.

"Sorry, Alderman, that wasn't my intention. Y'all have a good evening." Carl's partner drove the car on down the street.

After all the excitement Kiefer took a really good look at the woman beside him. Beneath the streetlight she wasn't at all like the person on TV, more like a college coed and less like a hard-nosed politician. Of average height, with midnight-black hair she wore pulled back in a ponytail. Her jeans had holes in them; not as a fashion statement but from actual use would be his guess.

His attention went to her tight T-shirt, which did nothing to hide the generous breasts but, in fact, drew attention to them with "not here you don't" written across them. What captured his attention was the necklace lying between her breasts. It was the same one that the woman he'd kissed on St. Patrick's Day had been wearing.

He looked into her dark eyes. Yes, those were the ones. He'd thought of that kiss and these very eyes many times since then.

"You!"

Ashley gave him a quizzical look. "Yes. Me."

She didn't recognize him. But why should she? He'd worn a mask.

Ashley put her hands on her hips and glared at the man before her. "What were you thinking?"

He blinked a couple of times as if he'd forgotten where he was. "What do you mean?"

Dr. Bradford looked truly perplexed. As if he couldn't imagine creating a situation that both she and he couldn't get out of. Marko wasn't someone to mess with. "Jumping in between Marko and me. I had things under control."

"Yeah, I could see that. Six against one is always a fair number. I was only trying to help."

What was it about his voice? Had she heard it before? That rich tone sounded so familiar. "You weren't. If anything, you were making matters worse."

Ashley clenched her jaw. She'd fought most of her life against being overprotected. To fight her own fights. After her childhood friend had been abducted it had seemed like her father hadn't wanted to let her out of his sight. For years she'd had to beg to walk the two blocks to school. Even when he'd let her she'd caught him or her brother following her. It had taken going off to college to break away. She loved her father dearly but she would never return to that way of life. Having this doctor ride to the rescue wasn't what she needed or wanted. She could take care of Marko and herself.

Dr. Bradford said sarcastically, "So, if I understand correctly, I should have just stood by while they scared you into doing whatever they wanted you to do, which, by the way, was what?"

"Marko doesn't want the clinic to open. He believes it's only here to keep tabs on him and his gang. You know, big brother watching and all that. What it amounts to is he's afraid that if the people in Southriver have something positive, they'll want more and stop letting him intimidate them. Push thugs like him out."

"That's what you want too, isn't it?"

"Yes. I want to make this a good place to live."

"Admirable. But if you're not careful you won't be around to see it happen."

That might be true, but she'd spent so many years feeling cloistered and controlled, as if she couldn't take care of herself, that as an adult she fought against it whenever it happened to her now. She wasn't that brave in her personal life, always questioning her ability to judge if she was seeing the real person. Fighting to truly trust. Her being fooled before had destroyed someone's life. She couldn't let that happen again to her or anyone she cared about.

"Look around you." She reached out an arm and directed it toward the buildings across the street. "Those were all businesses when I was growing up. Criminals like Marko slowly drove them away. I won't be driven out. This clinic is the first step in bringing people back."

"You have grand plans, Ms. Marsh."

"I believe in dreaming big."

"You have your work cut out for you."

"Maybe so, but when I ran for the city council I promised that I'd help make this area a better place to live and I intend to keep that promise."

"Even if it kills you?"

She shrugged. "It won't come to that. Let's go in and I'll show you around. Then we'll get to work." She turned toward the building. "By the way, don't ever step between me and anyone again."

Kiefer blinked. He'd just been put in his place by a woman who had been wearing a leprechaun outfit when he'd first met her. She didn't recognize him. He was a bit disappointed. Then again, why would she? Their kiss had got to him but that didn't mean she had felt anything.

And what was this about working? He'd been told this was a meet and greet. He'd made plans for dinner tonight. Something about Ashley's demeanor warned him that wouldn't be a good enough excuse for leaving early.

She walked toward the redbrick structure with large window frames painted white. It had a heavy-looking natural wood door that had obviously been refinished with care. On either side of it were pots full of bright yellow flowers. She looked back as if she expected him to follow her. When he did she pushed the door wider. After he entered she closed and locked it. Despite what he believed was her earlier recklessness, at least she was showing some caution.

"The building used to be a hardware store," she informed him. "This large area will be used as the waiting room." All makes and models of wooden chairs were stationed around the room. "I have someone, Maria, coming in tomorrow morning to act as receptionist. She's a good girl. Let's go back here and I'll show you what I have planned."

Kiefer didn't say anything, just trailed after her down a long hallway that had obviously had new walls built to create smaller rooms on one side.

"These are the examination rooms. I couldn't make too many permanent changes because I had this building declared a historical one so it wouldn't be torn down."

Was she a crusader about everything? Even buildings? He'd seen sound bites of her talking about revitalizing the area but he hadn't known that included defending old buildings. In his mind, constructing more modern ones would have been more effective and energy efficient.

"This is the supply room, where we'll need to concentrate our efforts tonight."

Kiefer stepped into the room. It was piled high with boxes. More than a night's worth of work faced them.

"What's all of this?"

"Donated supplies. You'll find they aren't hard to come by. Manpower is. People are more than happy to give as long as it doesn't require any real investment of time." She stepped forward and opened a box.

"Ms. Marsh, I'm sorry but I have another appointment at eight. I'll get started on this first thing in the morning." He had to stop looking at her mouth. Thinking of their kiss.

She made a disgusted sound. "I don't think you'll have time for that tomorrow and I have scheduled meetings so I'll be in and out."

"I doubt there'll be so many patients that I can't see to it over the next few days."

"You might be surprised. Were you told that this job would require long hours?"

"I understand those. I am an ER doctor. The issue is that I wasn't prepared to work tonight. I understood I was to come and see the clinic. Not set it up."

"Dr. Bradford, around here we all do what has to be done. Were you told you would have only one nurse?"

"No. I was just asked to start work here the day after tomorrow."

"You have the date wrong. Tomorrow is opening day."

He'd be there ready to go in the morning. She seemed to set high expectations for herself and others. Kiefer didn't need her reporting back that he'd not given his all to this project. He had to ensure this clinic ran smoothly.

Shrugging out of his lightweight jacket, he conceded, "I can stay for a couple of hours now. We won't get it all done tonight but maybe we can have at least one exam room operational. But first I have to make a quick phone call."

"Sounds like a plan, Dr. Bradford."

"Please call me Kiefer. After all, we have met before."

She tilted her head in question. "I don't remember that."

"Now my feelings are hurt. It was at a St. Patrick's Day party."

A look of concern came over her face. She studied him for a moment. "Really?"

"You invited me to dance."

Ashley sucked in a breath. Her eyes widened. "You grabbed me in the hall."

"I'm sorry about that. Heat of the moment and all that." Kiefer wasn't going into why he'd kissed her. He also wasn't going to let on how much he'd enjoyed doing so.

"I should have slapped your face."

He shrugged. "Probably."

Ashley's hands shook as she opened the first box. She glanced at Kiefer. He had been the one. The man whose kiss had turned her inside out. She'd pushed him away and had gone down the hall back to the party on wobbly knees. No kiss had ever lingered and stayed with her like his had. Even months later she could remember every detail. But could she trust him? Someone who just grabbed a stranger and kissed them?

Kiefer looked at her. She turned away. Was he thinking of their kiss? Worse, laughing at her? She had to get past the moment and concentrate on the job at hand. What they had shared had been two adults being silly during a party.

He wasn't who she'd expected, on more than one front. She'd thought an older, more established doctor would be assigned to the clinic. The council had only agreed to support the clinic if she could work out an affiliation with the Savannah Medical Center. Only when she'd managed to make the connection had the plan come together. The six-month time limit meant the clinic had to look good from the first day and there could be no issues, like with Marko.

Her next concern was that if the clinic did make

a go of things, would Kiefer stay and run it after the six months were up? Or would he be like so many others? All her life she'd seen people wanting to help come and go in her community. Civic groups, church groups, private companies, all wanting to make a difference. The problem was that they never stayed long enough to make a real change. Slowly the strides forward would slide back to the way they had been. They came in and did their projects for the allotted time then left, never really committing to Southriver. Ashley needed people who would stay and be a part of the community. Someone who would have the same conviction about the community as she did.

When she'd been elected from the Southriver district to serve as alderman, the establishment of close affordable medical care had been one of her main platform points.

*If there had been a clinic close by, Lizzy might have lived.*

The clinic was the first of many improvements Ashley planned to implement. The beginning of making restitution for not having been there for Lizzy. But she had to show success with this project before she requested funds for the next.

* * *

They spent the following few hours opening boxes. Kiefer would tell her where the supplies were needed and she would put them there. He was a clean-cut guy in an all-American way. Dressed in a knit collared shirt and jeans, which seemed worn enough that they might be his favorite, and loafers. He was a striking man. As much so as he had been on St. Patrick's Day. He oozed confidence, but she knew from experience that he would need to gain acceptance in this neighborhood. His eyes were his most arresting feature. They twinkled with merriment. She should have remembered them, but it had been his voice that had pulled at her. That timbre when he said certain words made it special.

Kiefer was a worker, she'd give him that. She had no idea what some of the items they were handling were or how they were used, but he seemed pleased to see each of them. On occasion she would catch him looking at her. It made her feel a little nervous. That kiss stood between them. Theirs was a business relationship and she was going to see that it stayed that way.

"I'll need to make a list of other things we need when we get this all finished," he said.

"Good luck with that. I had a hard enough time getting these donated."

"I know someone I could ask."

"Who's that?" Ashley pushed another empty box out of the way.

"My mother. She's always looking for a cause. I'll put her on it. It may take a while for us to get what we need, but we will."

"Your mother isn't Maggie Bradford, is she?" She should have known. Last name Bradford. She'd been at Maggie Bradford's party. Great. Another connection between them. Ashley knew his mother.

"That's her."

"She's a smart woman. Very persuasive."

"Yeah. That's Mom."

He didn't sound that pleased. "She has a big heart."

A shadowy look came over his face. "Sometimes to her own detriment. That's a characteristic the two of you share." He picked up another box and headed out the door.

What had he meant by that comment?

Sometime later he looked at the large, expensive watch on his wrist. "I'm sorry, but I've gotta go. I'll finish the rest of this tomorrow." Picking up his jacket from where he'd hung it, he pulled it on. "Walk to the door with me. I want to make sure you close up."

"You don't have to worry about me. I've lived in Southriver all my life and I'll still be here when you're gone. So please don't start trying to play hero."

"No hero here. Just put my concern down to having been there, done that, and humor me." He stood at the door, waiting on her.

What was that all about? She stopped what she was doing and followed him down the hall. Kiefer opened the front door. "Lock up."

"I will, but I'm going to wait here until you get into your truck. If any eyes are looking, they need to know you're with me."

He started toward his truck. On his way he called, "This lot needs a security light."

"I'll add it to the already long list." She watched him climb into his late-model truck. It was a nice one and she was afraid it might not fare well in this neighborhood. Vandalism could be a problem. It also made him stand out as a visitor, and that could cause confidence issues with the locals.

He waited with his headlights shining on her until she turned and went inside. Oddly, she liked his concern.

# CHAPTER TWO

KIEFER SPENT SOME of the late hours of his evening contemplating the curiosity of life. Who would have thought he would ever meet the leprechaun again and, even more amazing, be working with her. Life took funny twists. More than once as they'd stored supplies he'd thought about their kiss. Had that just been a onetime incredible kiss or would all hers be like that, causing that instant fire of desire? He'd like to find out but something about the all-business Ashley Marsh had said that wasn't going to happen. What a shame.

He arrived at the clinic the next morning a couple of hours before opening time. A group of young men stood across the street even at that early hour. A ripple of alarm went through him and his gut tightened.

Was Marko trying it again?

Stepping out of the truck, he used his key fob to lock it and walked toward the front of the building. The roar of a car going too fast filled the air. By the time he had reached the door the men had started across the pavement.

Surely these guys were just trying to intimidate him. Since the day he'd seen his mother beaten by the homeless man she'd brought home for a meal, he'd been on guard where people were concerned. He was a realist. Some people were bad by nature. Defenseless he wasn't anymore and he'd sworn a long time ago that he would never again watch another person be hurt.

Trash had been dumped in front of the door. Kiefer stepped in it to knock on the clinic door, all the time aware of the approaching group. His entire body was on alert as he formulated a plan if they attacked him. He vowed to get his own key today.

"Hey, you looking for Ashley?" the guy who led the men asked.

Kiefer slowly turned. "Yes."

"You'll need to go around back. The door to her place is there."

Was the guy kidding him? Kiefer counted heads. Four to one. He wasn't going to put himself into a position of being jumped. Before he had to make a decision about how to handle the situation, the door opened.

"Good morning, Dr. Bradford," Ashley said with a smile. She was already dressed for the day in a pantsuit, giving her a professional and approachable air at the same time. He recognized this persona from TV. The one where she was determined to get what she wanted.

"Mornin'."

She looked around him. "Hi, guys. Everything's okay. Dr. Bradford is going to be the clinic doctor. It opens today."

One of the guys said, "Okay, we were just makin' sure you're okay. Marko is spreading the word that he's pissed about what you're doing around here. We'll get that trash cleaned up for you, Miss Ashley." The guy dipped his head respectfully.

"Thanks, Wayne. I appreciate that."

Kiefer shook his head as if confused. Then, indicating the garbage, he said, "Why do you put up with this?"

"Because this is my home. I'm not leaving it because someone doesn't like me."

She was a gutsy lady, Kiefer would give her that.

Most of the women her age he knew were always looking out for themselves. How they could financially better their situation. Like Brittney. She'd certainly done a number on him. It had turned out she'd married him because he was a doctor and would be able to give her a good life. When she'd found out Josh's bank account was even larger she'd moved on to him. Now Kiefer had no use for women other than a casual night out and a few laughs. He couldn't trust one not to use him. As far as he could tell, they all wanted the same thing. What they could get for themselves.

"Come on in." Ashley opened the door wide. "We need to get ready. Patients should be here soon."

"Those guys said you live in the back." Kiefer followed her in.

"That isn't exactly right. The entrance to my place is there. I actually live upstairs."

"You don't mind living above the clinic?"

"It's my building and my idea. The people around here needed a place to come for medical care and I had the space."

Kiefer was impressed. She really was committed to seeing her ideas work, even to the point of financing them. Outside of his mother, few people he knew were that devoted to anyone other than themselves. How much Ashley reminded him of his mother made him feel uncomfortable. Did all her work to better the world leave Ashley with any room for anything more in her life? Did she have a boyfriend? Want children? Something to care about besides her political agenda?

That wasn't his concern. He believed in helping people. His mother had instilled that in him, but he was still aware that some people would take advantage of you. His impression was that Ashley Marsh hadn't learned that lesson yet.

She was saying, "I'm sorry I'm not going to be much help today. I have a speech to give this morning, a committee meeting with the local businesses and then a council meeting tonight."

"I didn't expect you to spend the day with me. I can handle the clinic. That's why I was given the job."

"I'd hoped to be here but these meetings were already on the calendar and couldn't be moved. I just thought I could help smooth things over with the community. My neighbors can be mistrusting until they get to know you."

"I'll be fine. I'll have a nurse to assist me, won't I?"

"Yes. Margaret will be here soon. She was also born and raised in Southriver. She'll be a great help. Well, I've got to get ready for my day."

Ashley left him and he started working on arranging the supplies they'd not got to the night before. Forty-five minutes later the buzzer sounded and he went to the main door. He checked out the window. After last night he wouldn't take any chances that Marko or his gang would catch him off guard. A dark-skinned, silver-haired, heavy-set woman dressed in purple scrubs stood there. He unlocked the door and opened it.

"I'm guessing you're Dr. Bradford," she said before Kiefer had a chance to speak. "I'm Margaret Nettles. I'll be your nurse."

"Nice to meet you, Margaret. I'm sure I'll be glad of your help."

She looked around the waiting room. "Ms. Ashley has high hopes for this clinic and I agreed to help because she's such a fine person, but I don't know that it's going to work out. I'll do my part and help you do yours. Now, can you direct me to where I can put my purse? We need to get started. You already have a couple of patients waiting outside."

"I didn't see anyone."

"You wouldn't. They didn't come across the street until they saw me. They'll be along in a minute."

He glanced out the door. "But we don't open for another hour."

"That may be so but they'll be here nonetheless."

Margaret was correct. He closed the door and showed her to the office. She'd just locked her purse in the desk when the buzzer sounded.

"I'll see to that," Margaret announced.

"I only have the one exam room set up. I thought we'd have time to work on the other two between patients."

"I doubt that'll happen. Despite some in the neighborhood being against this clinic, the people around here need it. They'll come until they're scared away. I'll put your first patient in the exam room." With that she walked heavily down the hall.

*What had he got himself into?*

A boy of about three was his first patient. The

mother didn't look much older than eighteen. Much too young to have a child. Her hair was pulled back, which added to her look of youth. The little boy was clean but his clothes were well-worn and a little small on his chubby body.

"Hello, I'm Dr. Bradford. What's the problem today?"

"Mikey has a bad cold."

Kiefer could see that clearly. The child had a horribly running nose and a wet cough. Kiefer went down on his heels. "Mikey, I need to listen to your chest for a minute. This won't hurt."

He placed the stethoscope on the boy's chest. His heartbeat was steady but his lungs made a raspy sound. After that Kiefer checked Mikey's mouth and ears. Both were red and irritated.

Kiefer looked at the mother. "Mikey's going to need antibiotics for ten days. Then I want you to come back."

The girl's face took on a troubled look.

Kiefer stood. "Mikey should be just fine."

"Is there something else you can do for him?"

"The medicine should fix him right up." Kiefer looped the stethoscope around his neck.

"I can't get the medicine," the mother said softly.

"Raeshell." Ashley spoke to the mother from the open door. "I'm on my way to the drugstore right now. Dr. Bradford can write that prescription and we'll have it filled."

How long had Ashley been standing there? Was she checking on him?

It dawned on Kiefer that the girl couldn't pay for the medicine. "I'll do that right away." He stepped out into the hall.

He would make some calls when he had a chance and see about getting a few drug companies to help out. A couple of drug reps owed him favors. He'd be calling them in.

Kiefer pulled the pad out of his pocket and wrote the prescription. He then removed his wallet and took out some bills. He handed them to Ashley. "This should cover it."

"You don't have to," she whispered.

"If I don't, you will. You can't pay for everyone that comes through here. We're going to have to get some help in this area."

"I hadn't given much thought to people's inability to pay." She shoved the money into her pocket.

"Well, it's time to do that."

"I'll be back in a few hours. Maybe you'll have a few minutes for us to discuss it then," Ashley said.

"I have some ideas of my own that I'll work on as well." Returning to the room, he told the mother, "Ms. Marsh is waiting outside to drive you to the store. Don't worry about the cost. It's taken care of. I'll see you and Mikey back here in ten days. You make sure he takes all of the medicine. It doesn't work if you don't."

"Thank you, Dr. Bradford," Raeshell said meekly.

"You're welcome. Bring Mikey back if he gets worse."

"I will." The girl gathered her child close and left.

By noon he almost regretted his words to Ashley earlier. He hadn't stopped once. There was a constant stream of patients, each with varying degrees of need but none that he couldn't handle. His worries about being bored were long gone.

Already Margaret was proving to be a treasure. She knew the people who came in and put them at ease. Maria, his receptionist, showed up around nine. By then Kiefer had already seen eight patients. Margaret handled telling Maria what to do, leaving him to see a waiting patient. If every day was anything like this one, working in the ER would look like spending a day at the beach.

Around two o'clock Ashley stopped in again. This time she was wearing a simple dress and sweater. She looked refreshing on a hot day. "How're things going?"

"Busy."

"I'm glad to hear it. I was afraid Marko might bully people into staying away."

Kiefer looked at the notes he'd made on his last patient. He was going to have to start a charting system. "I don't understand why he wouldn't want a clinic here. The police, yes, but the clinic, no."

"It's all about power and control. He's afraid I'm taking it away."

"Doesn't his family live in the area? Need medical service on occasion?"

Ashley brushed her hand over her skirt. "Sure they do, but he doesn't care. Look, I've got to go. I have that community meeting. I just wanted to see how you're doing."

"Afraid I'm going to up and leave, Alderman?" He gave her a pointed look.

"I can't say it hasn't crossed my mind."

"Rest assured, I'll be here when you come back." He wouldn't be got rid of that easily.

It was late that evening when Ashley opened another supply box and searched the contents. Having no idea what they were, she left the box for Kiefer to see to. Her afternoon meeting hadn't gone as well as she'd hoped. The businessmen were worried about retaliation if they participated in the block party she had planned to celebrate the opening of the clinic. They had complained about the cost as well. In her opinion, the neighborhood needed to come together, start acting as one, if they were ever going to make a real difference. She wanted it so badly and couldn't figure out why the community leaders didn't.

Her evening council meeting had gone better. At least she'd had the good news that the clinic was up and running. It had been dark by the time she'd returned home. She'd changed clothes once again and had come down to the clinic to start arranging supplies.

Kiefer was behind the nineteen-forties metal desk in the closet-sized office, dictating into his phone, when she went by. He hadn't even looked up. She'd been impressed with his treatment of Raeshell and Mikey, especially when he'd offered to pay for the medicine. Despite his impulsive behavior at the party, he seemed to be a stand-up guy since he had already put in a full day and was now doing extra hours. She'd been disappointed that he'd not stayed later the night before to finish up organizing the supplies, but he'd more than done his share today.

A few minutes later he joined her in the supply room. "Hey."

"Hi," she returned.

"It's been some day."

"It always is in Southriver." She opened another box.

"That would be a great slogan for your Welcome to Southriver signs," he said.

"I'll keep that in mind."

An hour later they passed each other in the hallway, she on the way to the reception area and he coming from the office. They bumped into each other and she fumbled to keep the box she carried from falling. Already aware he was a big guy, being this near him only emphasized the fact.

His hands covered hers, helping her to balance the box again. He looked at her mouth. Was he going to take advantage of the situation and kiss her again? Her nerve ends danced. Something in her wanted him to, while her mind stated clearly that it was a bad idea. He was a stranger and she had no business letting him that close. She was glad for the space when he stepped back.

He said casually, "I don't know about you but I missed lunch and dinner today. Would you join me for a pizza? I'll have it delivered so we don't have to stop work except to eat."

Was he kidding? No one was going to deliver in Southriver after dark. She chuckled. "Good luck with that."

"What?"

"Getting something delivered around here after the sun goes down. Too many drivers have been robbed." She shifted the box so that she could see him clearly. Kiefer really was a good-looking man.

"You have to be kidding."

"Nope. Give it a try if you don't believe me." She was going to enjoy proving she was right. She walked down the hall.

When she returned he called from an exam room, "Pizza will be here in thirty."

She stepped back to the doorway. "How did you manage that?"

"I have a buddy who's a policeman and his family owns a pizza place. He happened to be helping out tonight."

"I'm impressed." And she was.

In a short while the front-door buzzer that she'd had installed the day before went off. To Ashley's amazement the pizza had arrived just as Kiefer had said it would. She hoped he always used his powers for good. Following him to the door, she said, "Check the peephole first. Never open the door after hours until you know who it is."

"You really should consider living elsewhere."

That wasn't going to happen. She'd made a promise years ago and she wasn't going to go back on it now. "That's not going to happen. It would defeat everything I stand for."

Kiefer looked at her for a second then out the peephole. "It's Bull." He opened the door.

A man as tall as Kiefer but much bulkier stood there with a large pizza box in his hands. "Well, Kie, you're sure slumming tonight."

Anger flared in Ashley. That was the way everyone thought of Southriver. If a person was in Southriver then it wasn't for a good reason, one of many perceptions she was working to change. She stepped around Kiefer.

Even in the dim light she could see Bull's eyes widen and his instant embarrassment. "Ah, I'm sorry. No offense."

She said in a clipped tone, "None taken. That isn't the first time my neighborhood has been insulted."

Kiefer chuckled softly as he gave Bull space to enter and closed the door behind him. "Careful, Bull. She might take you out, gun and all."

His warm sound of compassion took the edge off the moment for Ashley.

"Truly my apologies, Ms. Marsh." Bull sounded sincere.

Ashley looked closely at Bull. "Don't I know you? Aren't you the officer who caught the guy robbing the café a couple of weeks ago?"

Bull squared his shoulders and gave her a look of pride. "That was me."

"I appreciate that. The Gozmans are nice people. They've lived here all my life. I'd have hated to see them lose their business because they couldn't pay their bills."

Bull grinned. "Does that make up for my remark earlier?"

She smiled. "I'll let it go for now."

It bothered Kiefer for some reason that Bull was flirting with Ashley. Worse, she seemed to like it. It appeared innocent enough but he knew from past experience that looks could be deceiving. Brittney and Josh had managed to conceal their affair for months. But Ashley was nothing to him, so why should it matter if Bull was interested in her?

That wasn't true. Somehow his reaction to their kiss had added an element he didn't understand.

"Okay, neighborhood hero, I'm hungry. How about that pizza?" Kiefer pulled out some cash.

Ashley wasn't his type anyway. He liked her high energy and understood her big heart to a certain degree, but her drive to change the world was over the top for him. Too much like his mother. If he was ever interested in woman again it would be less about commitment and more about enjoying life.

"Bull, why don't you join us?" Ashley asked.

"Yeah, do," Kiefer said, in a less-than-encouraging tone.

"Naw. I need to get going." Bull took the cash and turned back toward the door.

Kiefer opened it, letting Bull exit, and stepped out as well.

"Listen, man," Bull said, "you be careful coming and going around here at night. Also, you need to get a security light for that lot." He nodded toward Ashley's place.

"I didn't get much else done around here today but I did call the power company about that."

"Great. I've heard good things about what Alderman Marsh is trying to do but she has stirred up some trouble as well. I hope you don't get caught in the cross fire."

"I'll keep that in mind. Thanks for the pizza."

"No problem."

Ashley was waiting on him when he came back in. "I'm ravenous. Why don't we go up to my place to eat where there's a table?"

"Sounds good to me."

She led the way down the hall. At the end she opened a door he'd assumed was a closet. It turned out to hide a staircase. He climbed the stairs after her, getting a good view of her nicely round behind. When they reached the top they went through another door that opened into a small kitchen, which had obviously been remodeled. The brick walls and patchwork tablecloth gave the room a homey and functional feel.

Ashley placed the pizza box on the table. "What would you like to drink? I have soda, tea, beer, water."

"I'd love a beer, but I'd better settle for a soda." He took one of the matching chairs.

Ashley pulled two cans of soda out of the refrigerator.

"So how long have you lived here?" Kiefer watched as she filled glasses with ice and then poured the drinks over it.

"About a year. I bought the building two years ago and spent six months making it habitable. I still have work to do." She placed his glass in front of him.

"You did the work yourself?"

"All that I could. I had to cut corners where I could."

"I'm impressed. You've done a nice job, from what I've seen."

Ashley smiled. She had a nice smile. Sort of made him feel like the sun had come out. "It was a labor of love. And I do mean labor."

He flipped the box top up and took a slice of pizza. "If you don't mind, I'm about to starve."

"You need to pace yourself around here."

"Isn't that the pot calling the kettle black? You had meetings all day and still managed to check up on me." He took another bite of pizza.

"I wasn't checking up."

"Really? What would you call it?"

She shrugged. "Neighborly concern."

"We aren't neighbors."

"No, we're not. I'm pretty sure we grew up as different as daylight and darkness."

"You're making a big assumption. We might have more in common than you think." Kiefer leaned back in his chair. "To start with, we both grew up in a neighborhood. Are your parents still married?"

She nodded.

"Mine are too. We both went to college. We both have jobs that help people."

Ashley raised a hand. "Okay, maybe you're right. But I grew up in a low-income, racially diverse area, while I'm sure yours was an upper middle class, private school community."

She had him there. "Yeah, but that doesn't mean we aren't both interested in the same things. I certainly have a mother who showed me the importance of helping people. You're making life better. And I make people feel better. We have more in common than you might think."

"Now we've moved into philosophy. I think that may be too deep a subject for me this late at night." Ashley took a bite of pizza. Kiefer watched her chew. Was he ever going to get that kiss out of his mind?

"You might be right. I've been at it so long today I'm starting to feel loopy."

They ate quietly for a few minutes before Kiefer stood and pushed the chair under the table. "I need to do a couple of things downstairs. Then I'm going to head home. Thanks for the nice place to have dinner."

"I'm the one who should be thanking you. You bought the pizza and against all odds got it delivered. By the way, the local TV station is coming to do a story on the clinic tomorrow. They've asked to interview you."

Kiefer wanted nothing to do with that. When his mother had been hurt and the case had gone to trial, he'd been on TV as they'd come out of the courthouse. It had been a horrible experience. He had been the child who had watched his mother being beaten nearly to death but had done nothing. The shame had been more than he could carry. Since then he'd shied away from that type of attention. He had no interest in getting involved with anyone who was always on a mission. He'd been raised by a person like that, knew the risks involved.

"I'll see if I have time." He headed down the stairs.

Ashley was waiting for the TV crew when they arrived. In the last year, since she'd been on the council, she'd learned to court the media but to always be wary of them as well. She needed good press to help move her ideas forward in the neighborhood revitalization. Shining a good light on what she was trying to accomplish in Southriver would hopefully not only get the city council behind the project but set a precedent for what could be done in other areas of the city and other cities in general.

It was just after lunch and she'd only seen Kiefer a couple of times that morning. No matter what they were doing their kiss seemed to pop into her mind. The more she tried to shove it away the stronger it became. She'd almost reached the point that she wanted to kiss him again so she could put it behind her and move on.

Ashley had come down early just to check in and see how things were going at the clinic. Kiefer was busy with a patient and Maria was overseeing a full waiting room. At least there shouldn't be an empty room when the news crew arrived. She'd gone downtown for a meeting and had returned in time to grab a bite to eat before she was due to meet the TV crew. Sitting at her table in the kitchen, having a sandwich, she looked at the chair Kiefer had filled the night before.

He was a big person but had seemed relaxed in her small kitchen. It had been too long since she'd shared even a simple meal with a man. Most of the men she had dated hadn't been happy with the prospect of living in Southriver, and she wasn't interested in moving elsewhere. Her world was here and she needed a partner who understood that, who supported that part of her life.

Her one truly serious relationship had ended when she'd decided to run for the city council. He'd wanted her support to further his business but hadn't been willing to do the same with her desire to become an alderman. She had been crushed by his attitude. This was a man who was supposed to love her. It hadn't taken long for them to part ways. Ashley wanted her relationship with a man to be a partnership. She refused to settle for anything less.

Since then she'd made her views and plans clear in the beginning and they had turned off any other men she'd dated. She was starting to miss male companionship. Someone to just have fun with.

Could she and Kiefer become friends? Based on their kiss there might be some benefit sexually as well. She'd enjoyed her conversation with him over pizza. One other good thing about him was that he wouldn't be staying in Southriver long. No outsider ever did. Kiefer wasn't her type anyway. They could part ways without hurt feelings, she was sure.

But what if her radar was off? What if she was misjudging him? It had happened before.

Thirty minutes later Kiefer walked up the hall in her direction as she made her way toward the waiting room.

"So, how's the alderman today?"

She smiled. "Busy."

"Are you ever not busy?"

Ashley thought about that for a moment. "Not really."

"That would have been my guess. You know if you don't slow down occasionally you will burn out and not have enough energy to save the world."

"Save the world? I'm not trying to save the world."

"Sure you are. What you're trying to do in Southriver is to save a part of the world."

She'd never thought of it that way. "I'm just trying to help families in this neighborhood live better lives. That's all."

"If you say so."

Ashley stepped closer to him so that no one could accidentally overhear them. That was a mistake. She came to an abrupt stop. His aftershave smelled like citrus with a hint of spice. She forced herself not to inhale deeply. He didn't move away but instead he looked down at her. Her gaze flickered down and returned. They were uncomfortably close but she wasn't going to back away. "Dr. Bradford, your job isn't to evaluate me or concern yourself with what I do, but to run this clinic."

"Why, yes, ma'am, Alderman Marsh." He glanced behind him then leaned down as if he was going to kiss her and mumbled, "I believe your dog and pony show have arrived." He stepped around her and headed down the hall.

What was his problem?

She had one as well. He left her tingling all over.

Kiefer tried to stay out of the way of Ashley and the reporter followed by the TV cameraman. Maybe if he remained busy, which wasn't a problem because he was, he wouldn't have to be involved. He'd stopped by the office to make a quick note on a patient when Ashley stuck her head in the door.

"Hey, do you mind coming in to see Mrs. McGuire? She's agreed to let us film her. We'd like to get you doing the examination." She turned to leave.

Kiefer wasn't interested in being part of her publicity. He was a doctor and a professional. There were patients to see. He didn't have time for her PR show. "I don't think so."

Her head popped back around the door. "What?"

"I'd rather not."

She studied him for a second. "It'll just be for a few minutes. No big deal."

Kiefer shook his head. "I don't think an examination of a patient is a place for a TV show."

Ashley stepped farther into the room. "Why're you being so difficult about this? I need this publicity for the clinic. To raise funds that are needed desperately."

"I understand that but I don't think putting a patient on TV is the way to go."

The reporter came to the doorway. Ashley glanced back then returned her attention to Kiefer. Her face held a beseeching expression. "Please. I won't ask you to do it again."

Something about her look had Kiefer reconsidering. What would be so bad about doing his job and trying not to pay any attention to the camera? He did understand the need to shine a light on what was going on in Southriver. He said tightly, "Okay, but you'll owe me."

"Thank you," she said, then turned to the man behind her. "Russell, we'll go to the exam room now and meet Mrs. McGuire."

Kiefer followed the party up the hallway to one of the two functioning exam rooms. The camera crew stopped outside the door and allowed him to enter first. Mrs. McGuire was a forty-something woman neatly dressed in a casual shirt and jeans. When he entered she looked up from where she sat in a chair in the corner.

"Hi, I'm Dr. Bradford. I understand you're Mrs. McGuire."

Ashley, along with the reporter and cameraman, squeezed into the room.

Mrs. McGuire looked at the group with interest. "I am."

"Are you sure you're okay with this?" Kiefer nodded toward the people behind him. "I'll tell them to leave if you're not."

"Mrs. McGuire—" Ashley started.

"Is *my* patient."

Ashley said nothing more.

The patient nodded her assent. "Now, Mrs.

McGuire, what seems to be the problem?" Kiefer asked.

"I've been having trouble with one of my toes." She lifted her right foot. It was covered by a sock and she was wearing a house shoe.

"Would you please remove your sock? I'd like to take a look." As she did so Kiefer pulled the other metal chair in the room closer.

A sweet smell of infection filled the room. He reached down and cupped her calf, lifting it so that her heel rested on his thigh. Mrs. McGuire's large toe was a deep purple color that was extending to the next one.

The cameraman took a step closer.

"How long has this toe looked like this?" Kiefer asked, trying not to let his concern show in his voice. He didn't want the reporter to get the idea that this might be more than an ordinary hurt toe.

"Oh, I don't know. Maybe a few months."

Kiefer nodded. She should have been seen long ago. "Mrs. McGuire, have you ever been told you were a diabetic?"

"It's been so long since I've been to the doctor I don't remember."

Kiefer took a deep breath, trying to remain

calm. Why had she let this go on for so long? Did she realize how bad it was? He turned to the reporter. "I need you to leave now. I would like to talk to my patient in private."

"But we really didn't get anything," the reporter complained.

"Dr. Bradford, could I speak to you outside?" Ashley followed the reporter and cameraman out.

"Mrs. McGuire, I'll be right back," Kiefer said.

Ashley waited in the hall. He closed the exam room door behind him. The reporter and cameraman were walking toward the waiting area.

"Why're you making this so difficult?" she demanded, before he could say anything.

"Because that woman in there needs to be in the hospital. She's going to lose that toe. If she waits much longer she could lose her entire foot. I don't think that's something that should be said in front of a camera."

Ashley's mouth formed an O of comprehension.

"That's right, oh. Now, if we're done here I'll see about making arrangements to have her admitted."

"I'm sorry. I didn't know. I'll see that she gets there. I know she lives alone and will need a ride.

That's probably why she hasn't been seeing a doctor regularly."

Kiefer had to admit Ashley's focus turned quickly to compassion and willingness to help. Despite her appearance of having a one-track mind, only concerned about her agenda, she genuinely seemed to have the woman's best interests at heart.

She headed down the hall toward the reporter and Kiefer returned to Mrs. McGuire.

He took the chair again and explained the situation to his patient.

Mrs. McGuire surprised him with her reaction when she said, "I'm not going to the hospital. Nothing good happens there."

That wasn't generally true but in her case it might be. Kiefer wasn't sure if her prognosis might be worse than he'd anticipated. At a knock on the door he said, "Come in."

Ashley entered. "Mrs. McGuire, I'm going to drive you to the hospital."

"I'm not going."

Ashley's eyes widened as she gave Mrs. McGuire an incredulous look. "Why not?"

"Because I don't want a bunch of people I don't know poking at me."

"Please, Mrs. McGuire, you need to have your foot seen to. I'll be there with you. Didn't Dr. Bradford tell you how important this is to your health?"

"I did," Kiefer said.

"I understand the doctor is trying to help but I'll be all right." Mrs. McGuire started putting on her sock. "I'll just give it a good soak and it'll get better like it always has."

Kiefer leaned forward, capturing her gaze. "That might work for a little while but not forever, and when it stops you'll be in bigger trouble. Please reconsider."

Ashley placed her hand on his shoulder. He was far too conscious of it remaining there as she said, "Dr. Bradford, would you let me speak to Mrs. McGuire for a second?"

"Sure." He left. What did Ashley have to say that couldn't be said in front of him? As he went into the next exam room he saw the reporter and cameraman still standing in the waiting room.

A few minutes later Ashley stopped him in the hall. "If you'll make all the arrangements, I'll take

Mrs. McGuire to the hospital as soon as we go by her house and pack a bag."

Ashley could work miracles. "What did you say to get her to go?"

She grinned. "What's said between two women stays between two women."

"That's not been my experience."

She looked at him with her chin tilted to one side. "Why, Doctor, I do believe you're a bit jaded."

"No, I've lived long enough to know differently. But it doesn't matter. I'm just glad you convinced her."

# CHAPTER THREE

ASHLEY DROVE HOME well after dark. She'd got Mrs. McGuire settled in the hospital, but not happily so. Her only hope was that Mrs. McGuire would stay long enough to get the care she needed. Now having the clinic in the neighborhood, the older woman would have a place to go to for care. The clinic was already making a difference.

*If only it had been around that day for Lizzy.*

As she drove by the front door of the clinic she saw a couple of boys on either side of it. They were pushing over the urns. Ashley honked her horn and their heads jerked up. She recognized them as members of Marko's gang. Rolling down the window, she hollered, "Hey, stop that!"

That was all it took for them to take off running.

With a sigh, she parked and climbed out. She walked over to see how big a mess had been made. It was late, she was tired and didn't feel like cleaning it up. But if she didn't do it now, what was left of the flowers would be dead by morning. She reached the door just as it was opened. She almost fell but Kiefer's strong hands gripped her shoulders and steadied her. Her heart beat faster. She wasn't sure if it was from surprise or from the jolt of having him touch her.

"Y-you scared me. I d-didn't expect you to still be here," she stammered.

He let her go. Disappointment washed over her. Not a feeling she should be having.

Kiefer stepped out. "I was finishing up some paperwork and getting ready to head home when I heard something going on out here. I came to check it out."

She waved her hand around. "A couple of kids have been busy."

"More like Marko trying to make a point."

He was right but she wasn't going to let him know that. "I'd like to just consider it a prank. I've got to get this cleaned up."

"Can't it wait?"

"The flowers could die overnight." Ashley started picking up the plants.

"Ah, a woman and her flowers."

"What does that mean?"

"Just that women have a thing for flowers." He handed her part of a plant.

"You sound pretty cynical. Someone used flowers against you?"

"Something like that. Why don't you get the broom and dustpan?" Kiefer began picking up pieces of the broken urns and putting them into a pile near the wall of the building. "I'll get started cleaning this up."

It was nice of him to offer to help. "You've had a long day. Go on home and I'll see to this."

"I'm not leaving you out here by yourself after this happened. So forget it. Get the broom and dustpan."

"Don't tell me what to do."

"I wouldn't have to if you weren't so hard-headed," he retorted as he continued to work.

Ashley put her hands on her hips and glared at him. It gave her little satisfaction because he wasn't looking at her. "I am not hardheaded."

"You're sure acting that way. I've made a simple offer of help and you're still standing there."

"Are you always so bossy?" Ashley glared down at the top of his head.

He looked over his shoulder at her. "Are you?"

With a huff, she stomped through the door and down the hall. Kiefer's chuckle followed her. She hadn't enjoyed growing up with a father controlling her every move and she sure didn't like Kiefer telling her what to do. It was time to make that clear to him. She snatched the cleaning supplies out of the closet along with a bucket and returned to the front door. Kiefer had all the pieces picked up and the flowers laid off to the side.

"I tried to save your flowers but I'm not sure they're going to live."

He really was making an effort at being helpful. Maybe she could cut him some slack. "Thanks. I was afraid of that. Would you like to do the honors of sweeping or holding the pan?"

"I'll take the pan." His hand brushed hers as she handed it to him. A shiver went through her.

"I rather like the idea of you at my feet," Ashley said as she swept the dirt into a pile.

"Don't get carried away with the idea." Kiefer held the pan while she moved the dirt into it then dumped it into the bucket. "Maybe if we put the flowers in here they might make it."

"Sounds good to me." She went back to sweeping. It was nice not having to clean up all by herself.

A few minutes later Kiefer said, "I think that's got it."

"I'll carry the broom and pan in if you don't mind bringing in the flowers. You can just set them beside the door." Her body skimmed his as he waited for her to enter ahead of him. Why did the most insignificant touch between them make her heart flutter?

After putting the bucket on the floor, he said, "I'm going to call it a night. Lock up. I'll see you in the morning."

"Hey, you didn't even ask about Mrs. McGuire."

"I'd just got off the phone with her doctor when I heard the crash out here. She's doing fine. I plan to visit her before I get here in the morning."

He really was a good doctor. "Thanks for what you did for her today."

"No big deal. All in a day's work."

"It's a big deal to Mrs. McGuire and the people around here." *And to me.*

Kiefer nodded. "I'm just glad I could help." He grinned. "And I didn't have to spend too much time at your feet."

* * *

The next morning just after sunrise Ashley woke
to the sound of large vehicles pulling into the
parking lot. Crawling out of bed, she went to the
window and looked down to find a truck towing
a power pole. It pulled to the end of the lot closest
to the iron stairs leading to her front door. Behind
it was another truck with an industrial posthole
digger attached.

*What was going on?*

She'd been trying for months to get a streetlight
put in near the lot. More than once she'd been informed that it wasn't going to happen. Now all of
a sudden the power company was showing up. She
watched as Kiefer's black truck turned into the lot
and took a spot out of the way of the trucks. He
climbed out and walked over to one of the men
from the power company.

Ashley quickly pulled on a long housecoat and
hurried down the hall to her apartment door. Stepping outside onto the small iron deck, she leaned
down over the rail. "What's going on?"

Kiefer looked at her. "Harold and his crew are
going to put a security light in for you."

"I knew nothing about this."

"I called in a favor."

Ashley pressed her lips together. The light was needed but she didn't want Kiefer taking it upon himself to see that she got it. She could take care of herself, get things done without his influence. After years of fighting against stifling concern, she wouldn't let it take over her life again. She could grow to trust and depend on him. What if she did and he disappointed her? "I wish you hadn't done that."

He climbed the stairs. "What do you mean? You know this light is needed."

"I do, but what I don't need is someone trying to take care of me."

Kiefer joined her on the landing. She suddenly felt small and underdressed with him standing next to her in his golf-style shirt, tan slacks and loafers. He made her think of things that could happen between them that were better left alone. Her nipples tightened in reaction to his nearness and she crossed her arms over her breasts.

"What brought that on? You said the other night that you'd been trying to get a light installed out here and I just asked the hospital administrator to give the power company a call."

"Okay. I appreciate your efforts." She turned to go inside.

"You still didn't answer my question. What's the chip on your shoulder about people being concerned about your welfare?"

She turned to glare at him. "I spent most of my life with overprotective parents, especially my father. It took me a long time to break away and I'm not going to let anyone control my life like that again."

Kiefer's shoulders and head went back. "Whoa, I didn't expect that blast."

"Then you shouldn't have asked." She opened the door, entered and closed it firmly between her and the man who saw too much and managed to send her emotions into a tailspin.

Kiefer hefted a cement urn out of the bed of his truck. He was glad he'd backed up to the front door, instead of trying to carry it across the parking lot. It weighed more than he'd anticipated. The man at the garden shop had loaded the two pots for him. He had asked for their sturdiest and apparently had got his request. Positioning the urn beside the door, he returned to the truck for a bag of potting soil.

After Ashley's reaction to him arranging for the security light, he probably shouldn't be replacing the flowers without discussing it with her, but he'd not seen her again. She'd left just after daylight, that much he knew, because her car was no longer parked near her stairs.

He poured half the bag of dirt into the pot. What he couldn't figure out was her over-the-top reaction to him trying to help. The security light just made good sense. Was she one of those women who didn't want anything done unless she was the one to do it? She probably wouldn't like him replacing the flowers but she would just have to get over it. He'd tell her it was for the clinic and not her. That he was confident she would accept.

Why he cared he had no idea. After what Brittney had done to him he'd promised himself not to care about a woman one way or another and here he was planting flowers for one who wouldn't be grateful. Brittney liked flowers. She'd kept fresh ones in a vase all the time. It had turned out some of those had been from Josh.

Stepping inside, he used more force than necessary and picked up the bucket with the dirt and flowers he and Ashley had rescued the night before. Kiefer took a deep breath then headed outside. He was doing this during the only lag in patients he'd had in the last two days. Instead of eating lunch, he was out here planting flowers, something that was well out of his wheelhouse. He really needed to get a move on so he was done before a patient showed up. He'd handle Ashley's reaction when the time came.

That was sooner than he'd expected. He was in the waiting room, speaking to Margaret about how he would like the charting handled, when the sound of heels on the old pine planks of the floor headed in his direction. Kiefer didn't have to guess who the *clip-clip* belonged to.

Ashley joined him and Margaret at the old office desk being used as Reception. "Hey, Margaret, how's it going?"

"Fine. We've been busy."

"Great. At least we can prove to the council that the clinic is needed." She turned to him. "Dr. Bradford, could I speak to you for a minute?"

Kiefer didn't like her tone. It reminded him of when he was in trouble and his mother used his full name. Ashley must have noticed the flowers, on which he believed he'd done an exceptional job.

He followed her down the hall. She wore a pencil skirt and dark hose that made her slim legs look sexy. He'd always been a legs man and hers were some of the finest he'd ever seen. The swish of her hips did something to his libido as well. He shouldn't get involved with a controlling, political do-gooder. She wasn't his type and even if she had been he'd sworn off women. He'd been kicked in the teeth and wasn't going to put himself in that position again. Still, he could look and appreciate, couldn't he?

Ashley stepped into his tiny office. He joined her and closed the door. She regarded at the door as if she feared she might have made a tactical error.

"What's going on that you thought we needed to talk alone?" He was taking the offensive before she could.

"I, uh, I noticed the flowers out front. I'm assuming you did them."

"I did."

"You know that isn't part of your job description…"

Kiefer took a step closer and she moved back until her bottom was against the desk. He pinned her with a look. "I do, but it needed to be done and I wanted the guys that did the destruction to know that the clinic was here to stay. I also had the security light erected for the patients as well as you. Soon it'll be getting darker earlier."

She gave him a perplexed look. Maybe he'd managed to stymie her. Something she'd not been for the entire time he'd known her.

"I thought—"

"That I'd done it for you?" He took a half a step closer. There was that fresh-baked cookie smell again. He wanted to breathe deeply, take it in. He raised a brow. "You made it perfectly clear the evening we met that you didn't need my help."

"I guess I did."

Apparently when she didn't have the upper hand she could be dealt with rather easily. "Well, if we have that cleared up then I'll get back to my patients."

"Before you go I have one other thing to discuss with you." Her voice had taken on the tone of authority again.

"Yes?" He looked down his nose at her.

"Next Saturday is the community block party. You will need to attend."

"Is that a request or a demand?"

Ashley's eyes widened. "Why, I'm asking."

"That's not what it sounded like."

"Are you trying to pick a fight, Doctor?"

He leaned toward her. "No, I'm just trying to remind you that I'm not one of your subjects."

"S-subjects?" she stuttered.

Ashley truly looked as if she had no idea she'd become so wrapped up in what she wanted that she'd forgotten that others might have different ideas or plans. "I'm not employed by you. I like to be asked to do something, not told. Especially when it has to do with my spare time."

She huffed. "Would you please come to the block party?"

He acted as if he was giving it a great deal of thought before he said, "I'll be there. Do I need to bring something?"

"No, all the food will be taken care of. I just need the neighborhood to see you as part of them."

"I understand. Now, if you're through with me, I have patients waiting." He stepped toward the door, stopped and returned to face her. His hands cupped her face. "You know, it's time I get this out of my system." His mouth found hers. It was as sweet and perfect as he remembered.

Ashley made a small sound of resistance before she returned his kiss. Her hands went to his forearms and squeezed.

Yes, that fire was still there. Flaming.

He let her go almost as abruptly as he had taken her. She rocked back on her heels.

Ashley raised her head, giving him a haughty look. "I have an appointment downtown."

Kiefer opened the door and spread an arm wide, indicating for her to leave first. Her shoulder brushed his chest as she moved past him. A buzz of awareness shot through him. To make it worse, her scent lingered behind her. He licked his lips.

He enjoyed pushing Ashley Marsh's buttons. She exasperated and intrigued him at the same time. As for kissing Ashley, it was far from being out of his system. All he could think about now was doing it again.

Three evenings later Ashley was in her kitchen, preparing a simple dinner after a long day of ensuring that the plans for the block party were properly handled. She wanted the event to go off without a glitch, providing another step toward community solidarity and pride.

She hadn't seen or spoken to Kiefer since their last discussion. Or kiss. Boy, the man could kiss. Where the first one they'd shared had been hot, this last one had been steamy and delicious, and far too short. She still didn't remember her drive downtown.

If she was honest with herself she might admit she'd been dodging Kiefer. Something about him unnerved her. Made her want to let go of something she'd fought hard to earn. Could she believe in him? Trust him to be who he seemed to be?

She'd thanked him for the new security light more than once. It had been reassuring that she didn't have to worry about coming home to no light other than the one over her door. It was also nice to have someone to help her out. She liked it that he'd seen to replanting the flowers. Somehow it made a statement that the clinic and he were here to stay, at least for a while. But how long would that be for? Should she let herself depend on Kiefer? Dared she? She'd trusted people before and been wrong. Could she be wrong again?

His truck was still in his parking space when she'd come home. She'd made a point not to go into the clinic. Kiefer was correct—it was his domain and not hers to oversee.

As she chopped the vegetables on the cutting board beside the sink, she sang along softly to the love song on the radio. She stopped and looked over her shoulder through the arched doorway to the hall.

*Was someone there?*

It wasn't so much what she heard but how she felt. Seeing nothing, she started to place vegetables into the skillet for a stir-fry. She gave the pan on the burner a shake. Between songs, the creak of a board she knew well had her turning around. Marko stood in the doorway. She dropped the skillet, spilling half-cooked vegetables across the floor.

"How did you get in here?"

He had a smirk on his face. "The same way I go anywhere I want."

"You broke in." She walked to the center of the room and pointed toward the door. "Get out, Marko."

"Who died and made you the boss of me?"

"Marko, you know I'm not afraid of you." He stepped toward her. Ashley remained where she was, refusing to be intimidated despite her heart beating against her ribs.

"You should be," he snarled. "I own Southriver. Don't force me to make you pay."

"Don't threaten me."

He moved into her personal space. Ashley couldn't stop the shudder that went through her. She smelled his beer-laden breath as it brushed her face. He snarled, "I'm not threatening you. I'm making you a promise."

Ashley backed away until she butted up against the counter. Marko matched her step for step. He leaned in and picked up the knife she'd put in the sink. She sucked in a breath when he brought it to her face.

"I'd hate for you to have an accident."

"Ashley." Kiefer's voice came from the stairwell seconds before he stepped through the door.

Marko was already disappearing around the opening in the direction of her outside door.

Kiefer looked from him to her. "What the…?"

Ashley slid down the cabinet to the floor. Her

pulse raced. She put her arms around her legs and her head on her knees.

Kiefer wasn't sure what had been going on but it was too close to déjà vu for him. The situation reminded him of what had happened to his mother. In two strides he was across the width of the kitchen and looking down the hall. The outside door stood open. The screen was still slapping against the frame. He pushed the main door closed and locked it before returning to the kitchen.

Ashley still sat on the floor and he crouched down beside her. Gathering her into his arms, he held her. To his surprise she didn't fight him, instead buried her head in his chest. Soft sobs racked her body.

He brushed his hand over her hair. "Shh, I'm right here. You're safe."

They stayed that way for a few minutes until Ashley slowly pulled away. Kiefer let his hold ease but didn't completely release her. He brushed her hair from her face and looked into red eyes and a pale face. The strong woman he was so familiar with had disappeared. Compassion filled him. "Will you tell me what happened?"

She looked at him for a moment as if she didn't understand him. Finally she said, "Marko stopped by for a visit."

"There was more to it than that." He looked at the food surrounding them.

She gave him a sad smile and a little nod that reminded him of a young girl who had broken her doll. It was less about heartache and more about disappointment.

"He threatened me with the knife."

"He what? I'm calling the police." Kiefer reached in his pocket for the phone.

"Don't." She grabbed his wrist.

"You have to report this."

"I can't. I babysat him. Our families were friends. I wasn't crying over what he did just now but over the loss of that sweet kid, the one who wasn't so angry with life and injustice."

Kiefer leaned back and looked at her. She was an amazing person. Here she had been threatened with a knife in her own home and all she was worried about was the person who had threatened her. How like his mother. Where did they get that type of fortitude? What he wanted to do was kill Marko or at the very least see that he was put in jail. Kiefer had no compassion for anyone who treated a woman that way, particularly one he cared about. It had killed him to see his mother defenseless in front of him and here it was happening again.

"So you're just going to allow him to go around threatening people?"

Ashley stood. "He didn't hurt me."

Kiefer came to his feet too. "He might have if I hadn't shown up."

"I don't think so. He was trying to scare me."

"I'm not willing to take that chance." Kiefer glared down at her.

"I'm not yours to worry about."

He looked everywhere but at her, trying to contain his irritation. "I hope your big bleeding heart doesn't get you—or someone else—into real trouble someday." He needed to do something or he would really become angry. "Point me in the direction of the broom and dustpan and I'll clean this mess up."

To his astonishment she indicated a small closet door without argument. The recent events must have got to her more than she wanted to let on.

"I've got oil all over me. I think I'll get a

shower." She didn't look back as she walked down the passageway.

Kiefer swept up and gave a quick soapy mop to the floor. She'd been preparing a meal, so she couldn't have had dinner yet. He looked in the refrigerator and found ingredients for an omelet and salad. He was impressed with her well-stocked kitchen. Most of the women he knew would rather eat out than cook. Apparently Ashley dined at home often.

Ten minutes later he had put a simple salad together and still no Ashley. He didn't want to cook the eggs until he knew she was ready to eat. He went down the hall in the direction of what he guessed was her bedroom. The hall led into a wide room that had to be her living area. An eclectic group of furnishings filled the space. He'd bet his paycheck the tables had been yard-sale finds Ashley had refurbished. Was there nothing the woman couldn't do?

Small canister lighting and lamps gave the room a warm feel, but the fireplace with the white-washed mantel was the focal point. Two comfortable-looking chairs were pulled up close to it. This was a place where Ashley really lived. There was nothing pretentious about it. Down-to-earth and natural, just like Ashley. Two doors led off the area. He went to the doorway of one. It looked like an unused bedroom. He tried the other.

This was her bedroom. It suited her. A white iron bed covered in a multicolored quilt faced the door, with windows on either side draped in some gauzy material. A large free-standing wardrobe stood to one side and an old-fashioned dresser on the other. His mother would say the room was charming.

"Ashley? I've put some supper together."

There was silence.

He stepped farther into the room. "Ashley?" A whimper came from a doorway he'd not noticed before. Steam hanging in the air told him it was her bathroom. "Are you okay?"

A weak "Yes…" reached his ears. Through the fog he could see her dressed in the robe she'd worn the other morning and the necklace he'd seen at the St. Patrick's Day party. Did she wear it all the time? She sat on the toilet lid with her hands clasped together. Her body shook.

Kiefer reached for her. Taking her forearms, he helped her stand. Her lack of resistance indicated she was at the end of her rope. As he led her to the bed he said, "Come on. Let's get you warm and something in your belly."

He jerked the covers back, helped her under the sheets and pulled the coverlet over her, tucking them under her chin. "How about dinner in bed?"

"You probably think I'm weak," she mumbled.

"No, I just think you've had a shock and need to process it. You'll be back to your old demanding self in the morning, I'm sure. Now, you stay put and I'll have something for you to eat in five minutes."

"I don't want—"

"I'm sure you don't but I'm going to wait on you until I know you're feeling better."

"How did you know what I was going to say?"

"Because I know you. Enough talk. I'll be right back."

Ashley wished she could crawl under the covers and never have to face Kiefer again. How could she lose it like that? It wasn't like her. After her best friend, Lizzy, had been kidnapped she'd promised herself she'd never be in that position, vulnerable. She'd been in her own home and

Marko had invaded it. He had been right there before she'd known it. Was that the way it had been for Lizzy? Had she been as scared? She'd known Ron, just as Ashley knew Marko.

If word of what had happened got out, not only her parents but the neighborhood would be fearful. If the city council heard, it might be the end of the clinic. She couldn't let that happen. The clinic meant so much to her. It was a way for making up for the selfishness of her past. To compensate in some small way for her part in what had happened to Lizzy.

How could she have been so wrong about Marko? She would have sworn that Marko would never have done what he had. She'd believed that behind that bravado he'd just been putting on a show. In reality, she put on the same show. She didn't want anyone to know how scared she could be.

Trying to shake off the fears from long ago, Ashley pulled her covers close. She had to get control or Kiefer would think she was going nuts. Could he see how much Marko's visit had affected her? That was a joke. Kiefer had found her in the bathroom in the middle of an emotional breakdown.

Of course he now knew she had been scared wit-less. That she'd been putting on a front of confi-dence. What if he told someone and it got back to her parents? They would start in again about her living elsewhere in the city, even though they wouldn't leave Southriver themselves.

Kiefer was as good as his word. He returned with food on a tray. There were two bowls of salad and plates with omelets that looked perfectly cooked. The man had talents other than being a fine doctor. And he really was that. She'd been astonished at the number of people who had come to him for care. She'd imagined that the people of Southriver would have been much more standoff-ish but apparently word had circulated that Kiefer could be trusted. Did she believe what she saw enough to agree? What if he fooled her like Marko had? Like Ron?

"If you don't mind, I think I'll join you."

She nodded. "I guess so. You can have it all, as far as I'm concerned."

"Oh, no, you don't. You're going to eat too. I'll shame you into feeling guilty that I slaved over a hot stove if I have to."

Ashley couldn't help but grin at that. She scooted

up in bed, adjusting the housecoat so that it didn't gape over her breasts. "Okay, you're being nice, so I'll at least make an effort."

"That sounds more like the Ashley I know." He set the tray on the bed. "I'll get our drinks. I didn't trust myself to walk all this way without spilling them if they were on the tray."

Kiefer was back in less than a minute with glasses of iced tea. He placed them on a table beside the bed where she could reach hers. Afterward he handed her a bowl. "Eat up. It'll make you feel better."

Ashley wasn't sure that was true but she took a bite anyway. Kiefer started in on his salad with gusto and was soon working on his omelet.

"So where did you learn your culinary skills?" She had managed to finish her salad and was placing the empty bowl on the tray.

"I think 'culinary skills' is stretching it a bit. If you're asking where I learned to cook then that's when I was in med school. It was either learn or starve. I had to eat whenever I had a chance at all times of the day. I can do the basics. From what I could tell about what I swept up off the floor, you might take cooking more seriously."

She finished chewing the forkful of omelet that might have been the best she'd ever had. "I like to cook when I have time. I was raised standing beside my mother in the kitchen, watching her."

"So does your family still live in Southriver?"

"Oh, yeah. You couldn't blast them out."

"Kind of like you."

"I guess that's true." She and her parents did have that in common.

"Your family ever think of moving somewhere else?"

"Only once, a long time ago." Those had been dark days.

"What changed their minds?"

She concentrated on putting her plate on the tray. "Mother and Daddy didn't know where they would go. They had never lived anywhere but here."

"My family isn't much different. Even my first cousin, who now lives in California, still considers Savannah home. Once you have Chatham County sand between your toes, it's hard to get it out."

Their families might have that sand in common but outside of that they had to be as different as swampland was from a desert. "Thank you for the meal. You didn't have to do this."

He grinned. "Sure I did, if I wanted to eat."

"Thanks also for not making me feel more ashamed of my breakdown. Please don't mention this to anyone. It would upset my parents if it got back to them."

"Nothing to be ashamed of. You had good reason. And what happens at the Southriver clinic stays in the Southriver clinic."

He needed to leave. Kiefer was far too charming. She was also far too aware of her state of undress and of him being in her bedroom, sitting on her bed. She'd not had a man in here in so long that if he was any nicer to her she might grab him and pull him under the covers. After their last kiss it truly was temping. "Well, I appreciate your help."

"And that sounds like my cue to leave." The bed gave when he stood. "I already know what the answer will be before I ask this question but I have to."

*What was he talking about?*

"Are you going to be all right here by yourself?" He studied her.

Ashley met his look and said in a firm voice, "Yes. I'm fine now. I just overreacted for a few minutes. I'm good now. Thank you."

"You've already said that. More than once."

"Well, I am grateful."

"The problem is that you sound too grateful for you. That's why I think you might still be a little rattled."

He saw too much, too easily. She leaned forward and glared at him. "What's that supposed to mean?"

"Now, that sounds more like the Ashley I know."

"Now it *is* time for you to go."

He chuckled as he picked up the tray and headed out the door. "I'll be locking up behind me. You do have your cell phone nearby?"

"Right here." She picked it up off the bedside table.

"If you even hear a noise, call 911."

"I'll be fine. Now, please leave so I can get some sleep."

"Call me if you need me. Even just to talk."

"I won't."

With his back to her as he went out the door he

said, "I know. Good night, hardheaded Ashley Marsh."

Where was a shoe to throw when she needed one? She smiled. He'd managed to irritate her but he'd also got her mind off what had happened. Kiefer Bradford was a smooth operator. That she could admire.

Kiefer double-checked the locks on Ashley's front door and the one to the stairs going to the clinic. Even the main clinic door he rechecked. He walked round the building, making sure there were no broken or open windows.

How had he been sucked into a woman's life that was so much like his mother's? In the past he'd made a point to date women who were nothing like his crusading mother. Brittney was a case in point and look where that had got him.

In his truck he called his buddy Bull and told him what had happened. Ashley wouldn't be happy he had but that didn't matter—her safety came first. Bull said he would see that the clinic was patrolled more often that night.

Sleeping at Ashley's had crossed his mind but he had no doubt that she would have objected strongly. He wasn't going to pick that fight but he would do what he could to see she was safe. The woman was too self-confident for her own good. Tonight had proved it.

Around midnight Kiefer woke to the sound of rain on the windows. That was one thing about living on the coast—the weather could go from flaming hot to a strong thunderstorm overnight. He immediately reached for his phone and tapped in Bull's number. He answered on the second ring.

"So how are things?" Kiefer asked.

"A little overprotective, aren't you, Doctor? Have things become personal with the pretty alderman?"

"No, I'm just concerned. Nothing more. Nothing less. So answer my question."

"Everything is quiet. Last time we cruised by no one was around. There was one upstairs light on but that was it."

Was Ashley having a hard time sleeping? Scared and turning a light on? "Thanks, buddy. Please continue to check on the place."

"Will do."

Kiefer put his phone down then picked it up, placed it on the bedside table then picked it up again. What was the worst she could do? Get mad at him for waking her. Scream at him tomorrow morning for calling. He should check on her. Just to make sure she was okay. Or maybe to just satisfy his need to know.

He touched Ashley's number, which he'd programmed into his cell phone when he'd been given it as contact for the clinic. On the first ring she answered. There was a hesitant note in her voice as if she was unsure about who it might be.

"Hey, it's Kiefer. I wanted to see how you are."

"Do you have any idea what time it is?" Her voice was stronger.

That was good. "Yeah, about one a.m."

"Don't you know better than to call people in the middle of the night?"

"I heard a light was on at your place. I thought you might be up."

"How would you know that? Either you're standing below my window or having me watched." She paused. "Bull. I asked you not to tell the police."

"I told a friend."

Ashley made a sound of disgust. "Same difference."

"I just wanted to make sure you were okay."

"You don't have to do that. I'm not your responsibility."

He pushed at his pillow, getting comfortable. "After what I walked in on I wouldn't be human if I wasn't concerned."

"Why do you keep pushing it?"

He didn't want to go into that full explanation. "Because I swore a long time ago that I wouldn't sit by again while someone hurt another person."

"What happened?"

It wasn't something he talked about much, certainly not to a virtual stranger, but for some reason he wanted Ashley to understand. "My mother was attacked when I was a child."

Ashley made a shocked noise. "I'm so sorry to hear that." For the first time since she'd been attacked she sounded like herself. "No wonder you overreact."

"I didn't realize I overreacted. I thought I was rather calm, considering. So are you sitting in front of the fireplace or are you lying in bed?"

"This conversation has suddenly taken a creepy turn," she said in a light tone.

"I was only asking to gauge whether or not you were really having trouble sleeping."

"So now you can make diagnoses over the phone. Impressive, Doctor."

He liked this quick-witted Ashley. It would be nice to see more of her. "I can. If you're sitting in your living room, that tells me you're still rattled, but if you're in your bed, there's a good chance you're recovering and will go back to sleep."

"Well, if you must know, I'm in bed."

"Good. You aren't still in that robe, are you?"

"Now you're really getting personal."

He guessed he was but it was for a good reason. At least her mind was off what had happened to her. "You need to have on something comfortable to sleep well."

"I changed into a gown soon after you left."

Kiefer hated that he'd missed that. Whoa, that wasn't what he needed to be thinking. He wasn't going to get involved with Ashley on that level. They were business associates only. He'd sworn off women. Those with an agenda didn't interest him and Brittney had cured him of taking a chance on being used. But those kisses between him and Ashley pulled at him. Said there might be something there.

"Good. Then why don't you turn off the light and try to sleep? I'm sure you have a full day ahead."

"You think you know me so well."

He was surprised just how much he did know about her in such a short time. The interesting thing was that he found he really liked her when she wasn't on her high horse about how she wanted something done. "Well, enough." The sound of her yawn came through the phone. "Am I boring you?"

"Maybe." She chuckled.

Warmth spread throughout his chest. "Then I'll say good night, Ashley."

The click of a lamp being turned off reached his ear then a soft "Good night, Kiefer."

What would it be like to hear that firsthand as he gathered her close in his arms? He was headed in the wrong direction. Backing off was what he needed to do. Ashley had been taking care of herself long before he'd come along and she would be doing it when he was gone. Tonight was an exception to the rule. Period.

# CHAPTER FOUR

ASHLEY WOKE WITH a jerk. She'd overslept. She had been more shaken by Marko's threats than she'd wanted to admit. Sleep had been easier to find after Kiefer had called. There was something about his deep, smooth voice that made her feel safe, as though he was right there with her instead of miles away.

Now she was ready to face her day. There were arrangements to make for the block party and she had a meeting with the zoning commission to get help with some buildings that needed restoration on the next block.

As the day went on she settled down, no longer thinking twice about leaving the house or going about business as normal. Marko had made his move and as usual was all talk. She'd seen Kiefer a few times in passing but they hadn't had time for anything more than a casual hello, no real discussion. What that would have been about she had no idea. Still, she missed their talks—or sparring was more the word for it.

The next evening she was in the kitchen, cooking, when there was a knock on her door. Her heart picked up speed for a second. She put it down to still being a little jumpy, not over-excitement at seeing Kiefer, who had just stuck his head around the door.

"Hey, I was on my way out for the day and wanted to say bye."

His eyes studied her too closely. Too watchful for her comfort. "I'm fine, if that's what you want to know."

Kiefer stepped farther into the room. "Never doubted it for a minute."

She smirked. "I bet."

He put his nose in the air. "Mmm, something smells good."

Ashley turned back to the stove and stirred the pot of black-eyed peas. "That would be my supper."

"It sure smells wonderful. Well, I guess I'll leave you to it."

"Kiefer." She turned around just as he was starting through the door.

He looked back at her. "Yeah?"

"Would you like to join me?"

"I sure would."

She laughed. "It didn't take you but a second to answer."

"I only get a home-cooked meal when I visit my parents. But those meals come with an inquisition from my mother about when I'm going to get married. When will she be a grandmother? Why don't I settle down?"

"Why aren't you married?"

He gave her a pointed look.

"I'm sorry. That's one of those questions you don't want to answer."

"I don't mind answering it. I just don't want to talk about it at every meal. I've been married and have no plans to do it again."

"That bad, huh?"

"My wife left me for my best friend."

She didn't say anything. What could she say that would make that any better? He'd had his own issues. "That's tough."

"Yeah, it was. Now, how can I help?"

"You can get the knives, forks and spoons and

set the table." She pointed. "The drawer to the left."

"Okay. What about you?"

"What about me?" She looked at him.

"Ever been married?"

"No. Guys don't seem to like sharing their time with my desire to work for social change."

"Understandable."

She caught his look. "What do you mean by that?"

"Just that you're a force to be reckoned with."

"I'm not sure that's a compliment. But I'm going to take it as one." She pulled a pan out of a drawer under the stove.

"Where are the glasses? I'll pour us some tea."

He hadn't agreed with her. Did he think she came on too strong? Why should she care what he thought? "They're in the cabinet next to the refrigerator."

Kiefer had to reach past her to get them and his chest brushed against her back. Suddenly the kitchen became closet sized. Her hand shook as she moved a pot off a burner.

"Careful with that. You might get burned." His breath fanned against her neck.

She shivered, very aware of him being near. "If you'd give me some room then you wouldn't have to worry."

He straightened. "I'm used to worrying about you."

"I wish you'd stop."

"It's part of the job of being the local doctor."

Ashley poured the beans into a bowl. "Did you always want to be a doctor?"

"No. I dreamed of being a beach bum. I still love the beach. How about you? Did you always want to be an alderman?"

"I was going to be a great journalist."

"So that's why you're so good in front of a camera." Was she?

"I guess. I didn't know I was." She pulled the pot roast from the slow cooker and put it on a platter.

"You seem very natural. I hate it." He took the platter from her.

"I noticed that the other day. It just takes practice not to be intimidated."

Kiefer walked to the table. "I don't want to practice. My one real experience wasn't fun."

"What happened?"

"When my mother was attacked the TV cameras were everywhere. Always in my face."

She looked appalled. "You were just a kid."

"They didn't care. But enough of that talk. I'm hungry."

She grinned. "I've never known you not to be. Sit down and I'll get the potatoes ready."

He did as she requested. When all the food was in front of them she sat. Leaning over the table, he made a big show of smelling and studying the food. "Do you always cook like this?"

"Once a week I treat myself to an all-out meal that I prepare. I'm usually so busy I don't eat right, so this is my way of compensating." She picked up a bowl and handed it to him.

As he spooned out mashed potatoes he said, "Well, I'd like to get on your regular dinner guest list."

Warm pleasure filled Ashley. It was nice to have a man appreciate her, and Kiefer in particular. "I'll take that under advisement." She watched as he took a large hunk of roast beef from the platter in the middle of the table.

She filled her plate and glanced over at Kiefer. He was waiting on her to begin eating. His parents had taught him manners. Picking up her fork, she took a bite and he dug into his meal with gusto.

"This is the best thing I've tasted in months." He raised a forkful of meat.

Ashley couldn't help but glow under his praise. "Thank you. You know I'm not going to kick you out. You don't have to keep going on about how good the food is."

He glanced up. "I'm telling the truth."

"I'm glad you're enjoying it." It was nice to cook for someone who appreciated it. Kiefer was starting to endear himself to her. She liked him the more she was around him, slowly learning to trust him.

"So when you're not cooking or being an alderman, what do you do for fun?"

"Fun?"

"Yeah, you know when you smile and frolic. Fun."

She chuckled. "Frolic. You pulled that out of the vault."

"You've never frolicked?" He raised both brows.

"Sure I have. When I was about four."

He asked between bites, "So you do remember fun?"

"Never said I didn't."

"Okay, now we're talking in rounds. Let me try again. What do you like to do on your days off?"

"I don't have many of them but when I do I like to go to the movies."

"What kind of movies?"

"I like old romances. *Rebecca, Casablanca, An Affair to Remember.*"

He stopped chewing. "Now, that's a facet of your personality I didn't expect. I took you for more of a shoot-'em-up person."

Was he saying that she didn't have a soft side? Hadn't she heard that before from other men? The idea really hurt coming from Kiefer.

Her chair scraped the floor as she stood. Taking her plate to the dishwasher, she put it in. "Well, people can surprise you."

Ashley returned to the table for two bowls and carried them to the counter. A large hand slipped around her and placed the platter of leftover meat on the counter just as she turned. She bumped into Kiefer's chest. His hands came to rest on her shoulders.

"Hey," Kiefer said softly, compelling her to look at him. "I didn't mean to hurt your feelings."

"You didn't."

His gaze held hers. "I think I did. You don't have to be the tough guy all the time."

Her hands went to his chest. "I'm not."

Kiefer pulled her closer. His look dropped. He intended to kiss her. The thrill of anticipation made her heart rate increase.

"I know for a fact that parts of you are very soft." Slowly his mouth lowered to hers.

Ashley closed her eyes as his lips touched hers. They were firm and sure. Wonderful. She wrapped her arms around his neck and returned his kiss. How did he manage to make her brainless when his lips were on hers? She pushed up against him, finding solid warmth that she wanted to bury herself in.

His lips left hers. "Let's go somewhere more comfortable."

What was she doing? She didn't have time for a complication like Kiefer. If they became involved and then broke up, which they surely would because they were so incompatible, what would happen to the clinic? It would make their relationship extremely uncomfortable. Should she believe in him? No, she'd been misled before. Be sure. Very sure. Ashley pushed hard against his chest, breaking their contact.

Kiefer looked at her with questioning eyes. He leaned toward her again.

She backed away. "I think it's time for you to go."

"Ash—"

"It won't work."

"How do you know?"

"I just know. I don't have time to play games."

He continued to watch her. "What games?"

"You know, the one where we get together, we play house and then we break up. I don't have time for all that emotional upheaval." What if she was wrong about him?

"You got all of that from three simple kisses?"

Was she overreacting? Maybe so, but she'd been there before, and during this time in her life she didn't have time to be sidetracked by getting involved with someone who was just here temporarily. Who would let her down in the end. "That's the problem. Your kisses aren't simple. I'm sorry—I'm tired. I think it's time for you to go."

"I will, but I won't be going far." He went to the

door to the stairwell. Before he stepped through it, he looked back at her. "Just know that if it was up to me I'd still be kissing you. All over."

Heat washed over her. Just the idea made her blood hum. If he tried again, would she stop him?

Thursday evening Ashley was on her way home from a monthly council meeting. She'd drawn flowers on her notepad as Alderman Henderson had expounded on how too many funds were being used in the Southriver district and needed to be redirected to the infrastructure of the downtown where tourists visited. Ashley had heard it all before over and over. All she wanted was to go home and have a hot shower.

She glanced at the Southriver Community sign that had only been erected two weeks earlier. The sign showed the outline of brownstones with a river in the background. She hoped the signs gave the community a sense of pride because with that came ownership, which made a neighborhood strong.

As she drove up to the clinic she noticed the light was still on. Kiefer must have been working late. He had become a real asset to the clinic. The people in the community liked him. She shouldn't be so amazed because she did too. Too much. His kisses, though brief, still lingered. She bit her bottom lip. It still tingled whenever she thought of Kiefer's touch.

Seconds later she saw him step out of the clinic door and reach in to turn off the outside light.

A *pop-pop* drew her attention away. Not even a second later there was a *tink-tink* of something hitting the right front panel of her car. Was someone throwing something at her?

She saw a blur of movement that made her think of Marko. Another *pop* and the windshield cracked loudly.

*Was he shooting at her?*

*Pop.*

Ashley stomped the brake pedal, shoved the car into gear and leaned down over the console. Her arm stung. She must have hit the steering wheel. She felt a dampness there as well.

Before she could react further Kiefer was beating on her window. "Are you all right? Unlock the door!"

He was already jerking on the door handle as

she pushed the button to release it. He slung it open before she could sit up.

Kiefer's head was inside the car. "Ashley. Ashley. Are you hurt?"

"I don't think so. Was someone shooting at me?"

"You're damn straight they were!" His hand was around her, pulling her into a sitting position.

"Did they shoot at you?"

"No, he ran off. He was after you."

"After me?" She tried to look out the windshield. "Oh, look at my poor car. Insurance is never going to believe this."

"Forget the car. How about you? I need to check you out. Are you sure nothing hurts?" He helped her out of the car.

"My arm does a little bit."

Kiefer said a string of words that could blister faster than the sun on a hot day in August. "You've been hit." He put an arm around her waist, supporting her weight against him.

"What?" She held her arm to her chest. Blood started to drip off her elbow.

"Stay still and let me have a look."

She did as he requested. Looking at her arm,

she could see that there was a ragged tear in the lightweight material of her shirt.

Kiefer ripped the cloth, enlarging the opening. "Hey!"

"Hush, your shirt was already ruined. I need to look at this." His finger probed along her skin.

"Ow!"

"Sorry. Do you have any napkins or a cloth in here?" he asked, looking toward her car.

"There are a few napkins in the door pocket." Her arm was starting to really sting.

Kiefer reached into the side pocket and came out with a handful of restaurant napkins that she'd stored there in case of a spill. He placed them over her wound, applying pressure. It stopped the stream of blood running down her arm.

She pulled back. "You do know that hurts, don't you?"

Kiefer didn't ease up. "I'm sorry but it's necessary. I need to get you inside where I can see. Can you hold your hand over it?"

Her head was becoming fuzzy but she said, "Yes."

"Good girl. Let's go." Kiefer supported her as they walked across the parking lot.

The sound of a siren and the flash of blue lights came toward them.

She tried to pull away. "You called the police?"

"Yes, I did. Someone was trying to kill you."

"No, they weren't. I'm sure they were only trying to scare me."

He brought her back against him. "Well, as far as I'm concerned, they were. Enough talking."

The police car pulled in next to them.

Ashley, despite her best efforts, weaved on her feet. "I'm feeling light-headed."

Kiefer grumbled something and pulled her tighter against him. He called to the officer, "I'm Dr. Bradford. Someone shot at Ms. Marsh." He gestured to her car and where the shooter had been with his free hand.

Kiefer kept moving toward the clinic as the officer took off in the direction he'd pointed. At the door Kiefer continued to hold her close. She moaned. Her arm was throbbing.

"Hang in there, Ashley. I'll have you taken care of in no time." He pushed the door open. As they entered Ashley stumbled. Kiefer scooped her into his arms and stalked to an exam room. There he placed her on the table. "Do not move."

Ashley had never heard him sound so forceful. Even if she'd felt like doing so, she wouldn't after that demand. "Don't worry, I'm going nowhere."

In almost no time Kiefer had returned with an armload of supplies. He dumped them on the table and then tore into a box, pulling out some gauze pads. Taking a bottle of saline, he opened the top and wet a square. She hissed as he dabbed around the wound.

"I hate that it hurts but it can't be helped. Can you lift your arm? I need to see if the bullet went through."

Ashley raised her arm and Kiefer tore her sleeve farther. His fingers were gentle and careful as he pushed against the skin around the wound. "I don't feel any bullet but I can't be sure until you have an X-ray. I'm going to clean you up and then get you to the hospital."

"I don't want to go to the hospital."

"Even if I didn't think you needed to go, you would still have to. It's the law that all gunshot wounds be seen in an ER." Kiefer added more saline to a clean pad. "Let's get the bleeding stopped and you wrapped up."

Over the next few minutes Kiefer cleaned the

area around the wound and put a bandage around her arm.

"Do you think you can walk to the truck?"

She nodded but when she stood she was unsteady on her feet. "With some help."

Kiefer pulled her close and guided her out to the truck.

"What're you looking for?" Ashley asked, when he slowed to look around for the second time.

"I'm making sure that someone isn't out here, waiting to take shots at you again."

"The police are here. They wouldn't dare."

"I'm not taking any chances." He steered her to the truck and lifted her inside. On the way round to his side he called to the officer who was examining her car, "I'm taking her to the hospital. It'll be quicker than waiting for an ambulance. We'll give our statements there."

The officer nodded his assent and said they'd meet them at the hospital. Kiefer glanced at her and checked her pulse again before driving away. For once Ashley was grateful to have someone taking care of her.

Kiefer paced the waiting area of the ER. They had told him to get out of the exam room. Go have a cup of coffee. Like he wanted some. His real worry was that someone had shot Ashley. Marko had been bad enough, but this… He'd known the neighborhood wasn't the best but he'd never imagined this would happen.

He made another trip across the floor. Ashley could have been killed.

Not soon enough for him, Will, the ER doctor and an old friend from medical school, pushed through the door to the waiting room. Kiefer didn't give him time to speak before he stalked toward him and asked, "How is she?"

"She's going to be fine. Has a few stitches in her forearm. The bullet didn't hit the bone. It was just a graze."

"You checked her over completely?"

Will eyed him closely. "I did. You act as if you and Alderman Marsh have something going on."

Kiefer couldn't meet his eye. Maybe he was overreacting but the thought of Ashley being hurt sickened him. After Brittney he had no intention of ever having something "going on" with a woman. He liked Ashley and didn't want to see her injured—that was all. "We're just friends. She owns the building that the clinic is in."

Will nodded and gave him a look that implied

he thought there was more to it than what Kiefer was admitting to.

"Can I see her now?"

"Sure. She's going to stay overnight just for observation."

"Thanks, Will." Kiefer stuck out his hand.

Will shook it. "Come on back. But you have to behave."

Kiefer didn't dignify that statement with a remark. He'd been alarmed for Ashley when they'd made it to the hospital. Her head had been on his thigh and her eyes had been closed. He'd brushed her hair back from her pale face and quietly reassured her. The realization that he knew almost nothing about her clawed at him. That had been the way he'd wanted it until now. The less he knew the less involved personally he would be. The thought of her dying changed things. He wasn't going to let her push him away again.

He slid the exam room glass door sideways just far enough for him to slip in. Ashley was as white as the sheet pulled over her. He took her fingers in his. More than once he'd seen loved ones touch family members the same way. When had this woman started mattering to him so much? Slipped past his defenses? His reaction meant nothing. He'd be this concerned about anyone he'd seen shot.

Ashley's eyes opened but were heavy as if she would go to asleep again in the next second. "Hey."

"Hi. How're you feeling?"

"Like I got shot. Did they hurt you?"

"No."

"Good." Her eyelids fluttered for a second.

"Can you tell me your parents' names so I can call them?"

Her eyes went wide. "Don't. I don't want them to know."

Kiefer squeezed her hand. "They need to know."

"It would just worry them. Please don't. They don't need to know."

Kiefer settled into a chair beside the bed. Minutes later a police officer entered. "I need to take a statement."

Over the next half hour he and Ashley told their stories as the young officer made notes. Against Ashley's objections Kiefer also mentioned the vandalism incident and Marko's visit. It was so reminiscent of what had happened to his mother.

All those emotions had swelled in him. The blind rage of watching Ashley shot, the helplessness of not being able to do more, the fear that he might lose her. He wanted to hit something.

"We are aware of who Marko is. He isn't someone to mess with. Ma'am, you need to be careful."

"I will be."

"If there's any further trouble, call right away. We'll be making a thorough investigation of the incident."

"I wish you would keep this quiet."

"Ma'am, a shooting is serious business. You were lucky. You could have been killed."

Ashley settled back in the bed. "I know," she said quietly.

The sun was shining when Ashley's voice woke Kiefer. "What're you doing here?"

Sometime during the night they had moved her from the ER to a room on the sixth floor. "Sleeping," Kiefer grumbled.

"You look awful," she mumbled, as she started working her way into a sitting position.

Kiefer jumped up.

She gave him a quizzical look. "My arm hurts."

"Here, let me help you." He raised the bed and moved the pillows around behind her.

"Thanks. Have you been here all night?"

"Yes." He stood looking at her.

"Why?"

"You didn't need to be alone and you wouldn't let me call your parents."

They were interrupted by a doctor entering. She checked Ashley out and said that she could go home but that she couldn't drive for a week. Her stitches would need to stay in for ten days.

An hour later Kiefer picked her up at the discharge exit of the hospital. He'd been driving fifteen minutes through traffic when Ashley asked, "Where're we going? This isn't the way to my house."

"To my place."

Ashley squirmed in her seat. "I need to go home."

"No, you don't. Someone was waiting on you. You're not going back there until I know it's safe."

"You can't tell me what to do."

Kiefer glanced at her. "I can tell you. What I can't do is make you do it. But if you give me a hard time I'll let your parents know what happened. It's time you trusted me."

"That's blackmail."

He shrugged. "If that's what it takes to get you to take care of yourself, so be it."

Ashley couldn't believe she'd been shot. Who would shoot her? Worse, she had to stay at Kiefer's house. Her emotions were swinging one way and then another. She didn't know him well enough to be his houseguest.

She glanced at him as he drove. He looked almost worse than she felt. There was some blood on his slacks. He wore a green scrub top. "What happened to your shirt?"

"It had your blood all over it, so I borrowed something to wear."

Ashley was wearing scrubs as well. She wished she had her own clothes. Leaning her head against the car window, she closed her eyes. "I'm sorry I messed up your clothes."

"Not a problem. I'm just relieved you weren't more seriously injured."

She must have slept because the next thing she knew Kiefer was opening her door. "Here, let me help you."

"What did they give me? All I want to do is sleep."

"That's the pain meds. You need to sleep. That way you'll heal faster."

He kept an arm around her waist as they walked to an elevator. "But I have things to do. I need to call people about the block party. And—"

"What you're going to do for the next couple of days is take it easy," he said as they rode up three floors.

The elevator opened and they exited to face a metal door. Kiefer unlocked it and pushed it open. Ashley entered and he closed the door behind them.

"Why don't you sit down while I get your bed ready?"

"I don't need to be in bed." She sank into an overstuffed couch.

"Even if you don't, I do. A man my size shouldn't sleep in a chair. I want you in a safe place where I know you're comfortable so I can get some sleep."

"Who's covering at the clinic for you?"

"I have a buddy who fills in sometimes. He agreed to take a couple of days for me."

"Aren't you afraid for him?"

"Not really. They were after you. Whoever it was didn't even try to shoot me. And I've hired a couple of off-duty policemen to watch the place."

"I wish you hadn't done that. The people of Southriver are suspicious enough as it is. Another stranger only makes it worse."

"The clinic should have already had security. With the drugs and supplies in it there should be security. The two guys I hired are from Southriver, so that should help ease the residents' concerns."

"You've thought of everything."

"I tried."

He'd managed to make her feel childish and selfish at the same time. "Kiefer, I really appreciate you taking care of me. I'm sorry I'm such a difficult patient."

"It's understandable under the circumstances. You stay put and I'll be right back." He went through a doorway, leaving her alone.

It wasn't that Kiefer's place wasn't a nice place to stay. It looked like a comfortable enough apartment. It was in one of the old warehouses that had been converted to apartments. It had all the basics but outside of that it showed little of Kiefer's personality. It was as if it was a place for him to stay but not a home.

Her head dropped to the couch cushion and her eyelids closed.

## CHAPTER FIVE

KIEFER RETURNED TO the living area to find Ashley asleep. He grinned. The pain medicine had really knocked her out. She had a real thing about showing weakness and accepting help, even when she needed it. What had happened to make her so independent? Picking Ashley up, he carried her to the spare bedroom. Kiefer had given a moment's thought to letting her have his room, but he was afraid she would pitch a fit and demand he take her home if she discovered she was sleeping in his bed.

He settled her and pulled the covers over her, taking care not to move her arm unnecessarily. When the pain medicine wore off Ashley would be unhappy. Leaving the door open, he plopped into his favorite spot on the sofa and propped his feet on the footstool.

*What was going on with him?* Insisting Ashley come and stay at his home? He hadn't invited any other woman to stay since his divorce. He'd gone to their places, yes, but never had them to his. Truthfully, bringing Ashley here had more to do with his concern for her safety than intimacy.

But those kisses were personal. Each had been far too short. Far too right. He drifted off to sleep remembering them.

*Someone was watching him.* Kiefer opened his eyes. Ashley stood over him. "What're you doing out of bed?"

"I'd like to go home. I need some clean clothes."

Scooting to a sitting position, he retorted, "I thought we'd settled that. I understand your need for independence, but right now you need help even if you don't realize it. By the way, are you in any pain?"

"A little but I'm more worried about having a bath. I feel all yucky."

"We'll work on getting you clean but you'll have to settle for a shower. I'll find you something to wear. Then I'm sure you'll need pain meds and some food."

She continued to glare down at him. "Since you

won't take me home I might as well take advantage of your hospitality."

Kiefer wiggled his brows. "You haven't seen anything yet. I'm just getting warmed up."

"Hey, I didn't mean like that."

He chuckled and stood. "Nothing like having an appreciative guest. I'll get a plastic bag to cover your bandage so it won't get wet. I'll be right back." When he returned he said, "Come this way."

"Where're we going?" Ashley moved to follow him.

He wiggled his brows again. "My bedroom."

She jerked to a stop. "Why?"

"Because my bathroom is through there and I have a walk-in shower you can use." He stopped at the bathroom door and looked back. Ashley stood in the opening of his bedroom. "Problem?"

"I'm just not completely comfortable with using a man's shower."

"You'll be fine. I won't join you unless I'm invited."

She smirked and walked past him into the bath. "That won't happen."

"Let's get that bandage covered." Kiefer dug

under the cabinet for a roll of surgical tape. Finding it, he placed it on the counter. "I'm going to tape the bag around your arm but you'll still need to be careful not to get it any wetter than necessary."

"I know, Doctor."

"Hold this…" he indicated the bag "…while I wrap it with tape."

She held out her arm. He pulled a length of tape and secured it. He did it once more a little farther down. "I think that should be good enough. I'll get you a clean towel and leave you to it. I'll be right outside if you need me."

He pulled a clean folded towel from a cabinet and tossed it on the sink counter.

"I'll be fine."

Kiefer listened for Ashley as he went about finding her some clothes to wear. Thoughts of her naked in his shower were better left locked way. That was an involvement he couldn't afford despite the pull Ashley had on him. He was already far more involved than he'd ever dreamed he would be.

Because she wouldn't be able to raise her arm to pull a shirt over her head, he decided on one of his old button-up shirts along with a pair of sweatpants. Both would be too large on her but they were the best he could do on short notice.

The water stopped running. "Hey, you okay in there?"

"Yeah."

"Open up."

"Why?" She sounded suspicious.

"I'm trying to give you something to wear."

The door opened a crack and a hand came out. He dropped the clothes on her arm. The door closed again. A few minutes later a groan came from inside the bath.

Concern flashed through him. "Ashley? You okay?"

Another groan.

"I'm coming in."

"Don't."

The word had hardly left her mouth before he was standing beside her. Ashley had one arm in the shirt and the other wrapped across her. She already had the pants in place. They were too large but at least they covered her. "What's wrong?"

"I can't get my arm in the sleeve. Hurts."

"I was afraid of that. Let me help." He reached out to her.

Ashley put her back to him. The shirt fell away from her shoulder, giving him an enticing view of her bare back, the creamy smooth skin inviting him to touch it. He had to remind himself to treat her as a patient, to keep his mind focused on the task when what he wanted was to take her into his arms. "I'll hold the sleeve out and you slip your arm in. If we have to, I can cut it out."

"I don't want to ruin your shirt."

"I'd gladly sacrifice it for the cause of not hurting you."

Ashley inched her arm into the sleeve. "My, the next thing you know you'll be fighting off my foes. Oh, yeah. You've already done that once or twice."

"It's nice you recognize it."

"I might do that, but it doesn't mean I like it. Or want it to continue."

He straightened the shirt over her shoulder. "Need help buttoning it?"

Ashley gave him a pointed look over her shoulder. "No, I think I can manage that."

"All right. I'll go see about getting us something to eat."

Had she looked disappointed? As if she'd expected another suggestive remark? Good. Maybe he was getting to her as much as she was to him.

Unlike Ashley's, his wasn't a well-stocked kitchen. He was home so rarely and at such odd hours that he did little but sleep here. Having her here made him see how sparsely he lived now, since the divorce. As if he just existed. Compared to Ashley's kitchen, his was cold and functional.

He phoned in an order to his favorite seafood restaurant just a block away along River Street. When Ashley was settled again he would walk there and pick up their meals.

The *pat-pat* of Ashley's bare feet on his wooden floors reached Kiefer's ears before she joined him in the kitchen. "Do you have some water or something? I'm thirsty."

"Yeah, just a second." He reached into a cabinet and brought out a glass. "What can I get you? I have water, week-old milk, and I can make some iced tea."

"Wow, what a selection. I'll take water for now but iced tea sounds wonderful."

"How does the arm feel?" He went to the refrigerator and used the ice dispenser.

"I would be lying if I said it didn't hurt. I still can't believe someone shot at me." She took a seat at the table.

He handed the filled glass to her. "Well, believe it."

"I really need to go home. Tomorrow is the block party. I have a list of things to do. Need to be doing."

"Don't you have a committee that's overseeing the event?"

Ashley drank half the water. "Yes, but I need to make sure everything gets done."

"No, *you* need to be in control. Why is that?"

She straightened her shoulders. "I don't. I just want things to go off without a hitch."

Kiefer sighed in exasperation and leaned a hip against the counter, studying her. "Well, I would recommend you request a police presence."

"If I did it would defeat everything I'm trying to accomplish. Too many police make it look like we have problems."

"Too few gives the criminals a chance to cause trouble. Again, why're you pushing so hard? I know you grew up in Southriver, but what you're trying to do consumes you to the point of being unsafe. You take chances and can talk of nothing else but what you are trying to do in Southriver. Don't you ever take a minute just to rest or have fun? Are you using Southriver as a stepping-stone to a state position? What drives you?"

Her eyes widened and mouth went slack. It appeared she couldn't believe he'd asked those questions. Had no one ever pointed that out to her?

Ashley clasped her hands in her lap in an effort to contain her resentment. She was trying to better Southriver for everyone. Her jaw tightened. Kiefer's implication that the work she was doing was self-motivated irritated her. How dared he?

She met his look and reached for the necklace around her neck. "It's none of your business what motivates me, but I'm going to tell you anyway." Although she worked to control her emotions, the moment she opened her mouth they came flooding out with her words. "When I was younger Lizzy, my best friend in elementary school, was abducted by the boy who lived next door to me. We knew him. He even babysat me and my brother when our parents and his went out for dinner. We all trusted him. Adored him.

"Lizzy knew him too because of all the time she spent at our house. We both thought he hung the moon, but one day when she was walking home from school he dragged her into the woods. He raped and beat her. By the time she was found Lizzy was in such a bad condition that she died on the way to the hospital. They said that if she'd had access to closer medical care she might have made it."

She didn't look at him as she continued. "I felt so guilty. Because of me Lizzy was by herself that day. I was supposed to go home with her but I didn't for my own selfish reasons. She trusted Ron because of me. After that the entire community was terrified for their children. My father never let me outside to play without someone watching me. I couldn't walk home from the family store by myself. I was so overprotected I was smothered. I understood why but that didn't mean I liked it.

"When I had a chance to go to college I was so glad to leave. But I missed my home and came back hoping to make a difference. Make it a safer place. I ran on the platform of improving the neighborhood. Headway is starting to be made and I won't, *can't*, let it slip backward. It's not about me—it's about making this a better place to live for everyone. Especially the children. I can have fun later."

"I'm sorry about your friend. That must have been a horrible time for you. At least now I understand why the clinic is so important to you."

"You have no idea."

A stricken look filled his eyes. He'd mentioned his mother being attacked when he'd been a child, but was there more to the story than he'd told her?

"Our meal should be ready. I'm just going down to Ship and Shore Seafood. Will you be okay here for a few minutes by yourself?"

For someone who was so insistent that she share so much about herself, he sure had dropped the conversation fast when it came to his turn. She nodded. "I'll be fine."

His eyes narrowed. "I can trust you to be here when I return?"

"I'll be here. I'll make iced tea while you're gone—how about that?"

"Great. I'll see you in a few." He headed out the door.

Ashley had the tea steeping when he returned twenty minutes later. She'd also taken the time while he was gone to call a couple of people about the block party. Thankfully it seemed as if everything was running smoothly.

Less than an hour later she took a deep swig of her tea and placed the glass on the coffee table. "Either that was the best meal I've ever eaten or I was super hungry."

Kiefer grinned. "My guess is that it's a little of both."

The sound of a tugboat horn drew Ashley's attention. She looked toward the window.

"Would you like to have our dessert out on the balcony?" Kiefer pushed his chair back.

"There's dessert?"

"Sure there is. What kind of host do you think I am?"

She gave him a questionable look. "I don't think you want me to comment on what some would consider kidnapping."

There was a tense moment as she registered what she had said. Surely he didn't think she was putting him on the same level as the guy who had taken Lizzy?

"You do know you can leave anytime you wish?"

She nodded. "I do. Perhaps I shouldn't have said that in light of what we had been talking about."

"I'll get our dessert."

Opening the narrow French doors, she stepped out on the iron balcony hanging over the cobblestone road below. She eased into one of the cushioned wicker chairs with matching footstools. Crossing her arms across her breasts, Ashley put her feet up and rested one ankle atop the other. A foghorn blew again as a barge slowly moved over the water of the Savannah River in front of her.

Kiefer joined her, taking the other chair. "Here you go."

She took the round plastic-covered disk he offered. "A praline."

"The best in the world are made here."

Ashley unwrapped it and took a bite of the sugary disk with a pecan in the center. "Mmm. Wonderful. Thank you."

"You're welcome."

Looking out at the river, she said, "You have a great view."

"It's the one thing I really like about living here. I spend what little time I'm home sitting out here."

"You don't like the rest of the place?"

"I got it in the divorce." Disgust and resignation sharpened his voice.

"Why don't you sell it? This is prime real estate."

"At one time I wouldn't do it because she wanted it. Now I need a place to live."

"So you live here out of spite." Ashley glanced at him from beneath lowered lids.

"The way you say it makes me sound rather small."

That wasn't her intent but he obviously wasn't moving on. "You said it, not me."

"Brittney left me for someone who could give her more prestige, fancier cars and a larger house." He couldn't keep the bitterness from his voice.

Ashley sat forward and looked him straight in the eyes. "No, she didn't. She left you because she is a self-centered, money-hungry, shallow person."

Kiefer sat back in the cushion of the chair as if she'd hit him with her outburst. "I've never really thought about it like that." Somehow hearing it said with such authority made him believe it.

"Well, you should."

"They were at the St. Patrick's Day party. I saw

them coming down the hall just as I was passing you."

"So that's what brought on that kiss."

Kiefer looked at her. "I'm not proud of it but I used you. I won't say I'm sorry I did because that kiss made my day."

She watched him for a moment before she said, "I'm getting tired. I think I'll go lie down for a while."

Had he said too much and run her off? "You need a pain pill before you do."

Ashley struggled to stand. Kiefer hurried to place a hand under her uninjured arm to help her. She stepped away from him. "Thank you, Doc. I think I can take care of myself from here. I saw the medicine on my bedside table."

"Call me if you need me."

"I'm sure I won't." What would it be like if she let herself need and trust Kiefer? No, it might change her life forever. Relying on someone was more than she was willing to take a chance on.

It was late afternoon and Kiefer was again sitting outside on the balcony. He'd spent the last few hours looking over paperwork sent over from the clinic and making phone calls. The first of those had been to a couple of drug representatives whose companies had an indigent program for people who couldn't afford care. Both had agreed to look into what they could do to help with providing medicines for the clinic.

The next one had been to his mother. He'd listened patiently as she'd reminded him that he needed to visit more often now that he was closer. He'd promised he would soon. With her placated, he'd asked her about helping to raise money for supplies for the clinic. As always, his mother had been excited about having another project to focus her energy on.

"So how do you like Ashley Marsh, honey?"

"She's doing good things in Southriver."

"That sounds like you're evading the question."

"I'm not."

"You know Ashley attended my St. Patrick's Day fund-raiser. Y'all didn't happen to meet there, did you?"

"We might have." That was an understatement. Thoughts of their kiss still slipped in right before he went to sleep each night.

"I would think that after seeing and speaking to her you would have more to say."

He did but they weren't words to share with his mother. "She can be difficult, demanding and exasperating, but she really wants to help Southriver. She's doing good things for the community. And, yes, she is attractive. And, no, Mother, I'm not thinking about getting married or having children." *Ever again.*

"She's a pistol. I'll give her that." His mother sounded impressed.

"Kind of reminds me of you." Ashley and his mother did have a great deal in common. Almost uncomfortably so.

"I'll be by to check out the clinic sometime next week and see what I can do to help. I'll call first."

"Thanks, Mom. I knew I could count on you." Despite what had happened to his mother, she had not ceased her efforts to help the less fortunate. Again, not unlike Ashley, who didn't seem deterred by what had taken place in her life. He seemed the one most shaken by both events. He still relived the horror of seeing his mother hurt anytime he saw or heard of a woman being threatened. Maybe that was why Ashley had got under his skin.

Kiefer went to the kitchen for another cup of coffee. On his way back outside he stopped in to check on Ashley. She was still curled under the covers. Her dark hair was a mass around her head. It was the first time he'd ever seen her truly at ease. Did she wear that same look of peace after making love? He'd like to give her that and more. But Ashley wasn't a good-time kind of girl. She would be all about permanence, something he wasn't willing to try again.

He backed out of the doorway. That was a place he had no business going. Based on the devotion Ashley showed her community and city, her relationships with men wouldn't be shallow and short lasting. She would give her entire heart to the man she was involved with and, worse, would expect the same depth of commitment in return. He couldn't give that. Wouldn't take the chance on rejection again. Yet the more he was around Ashley the more he wondered if it might be worth the risk.

Her statement about Brittney and Josh implied she had been angry on his behalf. Why would it matter to her how he had been treated? All he'd ever comprehended was that he had been betrayed under his nose by the two people he'd cared about most. Not why. He'd never thought that through. It wasn't about him but them. They were the ones with the issues. He'd just got caught up in their selfish wants and needs. Why hadn't he seen it that clearly before?

The sun had sunk to the point it was brushing the buildings with gold when Ashley joined him on the balcony. He'd been aware of her approaching even before he saw her. It was almost as if his body was in tune with hers. What was it about Ashley that touched him on levels he didn't understand? Didn't want to.

"Hey," she said timidly, which was completely out of character for her.

"Hi, there, sleepyhead. Feeling better?"

She slightly moved her arm, still in the sling. "It's pretty stiff."

"If you think so now, wait until tomorrow."

"Yeah, and I have the block party tomorrow."

"Join me." He nodded toward a chair.

Ashley slowly took the chair beside him. "I can't get over how wonderful this view is."

"Isn't there a place in Southriver where you have a view over the river or to the east?"

She thought for a second. "Yeah, there's one building but it's so run-down…I'd love to see it bought and redone into lofts like yours. It would encourage new people to move in."

"Your mind is always thinking about how to make Southriver better. Do you ever think about yourself? About a personal life?" She looked at him. Was she thinking about how poor his relationship track record was?

She propped her feet on the stool, getting comfortable. "I've had a personal life. My parents wanted me to live somewhere different. Raise their grandchildren where they wouldn't have to worry about them. I almost married right out of college. But it turned out he wasn't interested in my running for political office and he started running around on me. I decided then I was better off alone, doing my own thing."

"Not every man is disloyal."

She looked at him. "No, some just go around kissing strangers at parties."

"I explained that."

"You did." She looked into the distance. "Women

like to be wanted for themselves, not as a way to hide from ex-wives."

"Okay, I deserve that, but in my defense the next ones were all about wanting to kiss you." He watched as pink found Ashley's cheeks.

She smiled and said quietly, "Thank you."

He'd put her on the spot enough. "Hungry?"

"I'm fine. You don't have to fuss over me. Is there any chance you'll take me home this evening?"

"Nope."

"You know you can't hold me hostage forever." Thankfully her tone was teasing rather than irritated. She didn't feel threatened if she was making a joke.

The last ray of daylight touched her face and the glow made her beautiful. He murmured, "You and I both know you could leave if you really wanted to."

Ashley shifted slightly in her chair but didn't look at him. "I need to be home in time to get ready for the block party. We both have to attend."

"Not a problem. I'll have you to your place first thing in the morning."

They settled into silence as the stars slowly

began to come out. Kiefer couldn't remember the last time he'd been completely comfortable not saying a word when spending time with someone. There was something special about that.

Arms held Ashley. She pushed at them. "Stop, stop."

A large hand shook her shoulder. "Ashley, shush. You're safe. You're just dreaming."

The bed shifted and she was pulled against something firm and warm. All her fear faded away. Snuggling against the wall, she found sleep again, feeling secure and protected.

Suddenly awake again, she kicked at the covers, her foot making contact with a hard leg. At a loud *"Ow!"* her eyes flashed open. Kiefer rubbed his thigh.

"What're you doing here?" It was still dark. Ashley could barely make out his form stretched along her bed. Kiefer's arm was under her neck and her cheek rested on his shoulder. His other arm was across her waist.

He gently patted her hip. "You were having a bad dream. Now, hush and go back to sleep."

For a fleeting second Ashley started to order him to get out of her bed, but the temptation to snuggle back against his heat and continue to sleep was too great. She succumbed to that desire and closed her eyes once more.

The next time Ashley woke she blinked against the sunlight streaming through the windows. She lay on her side with her bad arm supported by the bare midsection of a muscular male body. She looked down to see athletic shorts at his waist.

He muttered, "Yes. You're draped across me."

*How did Kiefer know what she was going to say?* She moved enough that she could look at him. "What're you doing in my bed?"

"Still asking the same old question? Don't you remember me answering that last night? You had a bad dream. I came in to see if you were okay."

"And stayed." Her body tensed and her tone questioned his motives.

He shrugged, showing no shame. "Something like that."

Ashley jerked to a sitting position and groaned as pain exploded through her arm. She grabbed it and held it close. "What time is it?"

Kiefer twisted to look toward the clock on the bedside table. "Six forty-five."

"We've got to go. I've a lot to do." Ashley was already moving toward her side of the bed.

A gentle hand circled the wrist of her uninjured arm. "Hold up a minute. I need to have a look at that bandage."

"It can wait. I need to get a bath." She looked down at her clothing. "I need to change my clothes. I have to make my dish to take. I also have to be there to organize the tables and see that the media gets the story correct."

Kiefer put up a hand. "Whoa, whoa. You were shot the day before yesterday and you still need to take it easy. I'll help you with what you need to do but your health comes first. I'll cover the arm and you can get a shower. Then I'll put a new bandage on it. I had Margaret send over some clothes for you, but I'm sure they aren't what you want to wear to the block party, so after stopping by Home Cookin' Restaurant for a gallon of potato salad, we'll go to your place so you can change."

Ashley gave him a blunt look. "Are you about finished organizing me?"

He dipped his chin and pushed himself up to lean back against the headboard, giving her an enticing view of male chest, enough that she almost lost her train of thought.

"Yes," Kiefer said.

"I'd rather just leave now for my house."

"I'm the one doing the driving, so I'm the one with the plan."

She could argue further but it would only take up valuable time. Based on Kiefer's body language and his tone of voice, things were going to happen the way he'd decided. "Okay, you win. Let's get this arm ready for the shower."

She watched Kiefer rise lithely from the bed. "I'll get a new bag and meet you in my bathroom."

That sounded sort of kinky. Why was she thinking that? Maybe because she'd awakened in his arms. She had to quit having such thoughts about Kiefer. She needed someone that would be with her for the long haul, a man she could trust to be there for her always. He didn't want a long-term relationship and she couldn't agree to anything less. He'd also made it clear he wasn't impressed by Southriver.

She must have made a face because he asked, "Problem?"

The man was far too perceptive. "No," she croaked.

His look implied he didn't believe her. "Okay, see you in a sec in the bath."

Ashley watched the half-clothed man go out the door as if he had no idea what he was doing to her. Ashley swallowed hard. There it was again. The suggestion, even in her mind, made her tingle all over. He probably wasn't aware of his physical effect on her. For all she knew, he had women over all the time.

She left the bed with a groan. Her arm was so stiff. Moving it gently, she worked some of the ache out. On bare feet she made her way to Kiefer's room. His bedcovers looked as if he had been asleep and had thrown them back in a hurry. She must have cried out and alarmed him.

"You'll need to take that shirt off." He entered the bathroom.

She turned her back to him.

"Come on. I'm a doctor. I've seen plenty of naked bodies."

Ashley removed her arm from the sleeve with a fair amount of pain. Pulling one side of the shirt over the other to cover her breasts, she presented her arm to him. "You're not my doctor and you haven't seen mine."

Kiefer met her gaze. "But I'd like to."

Heat washed over her and her knees went weak. That shouldn't be happening. Kiefer wasn't who she wanted. Certainly not who she needed. "Dr. Bradford, are you trying to take advantage of the situation?"

"Maybe, but it's the truth. Right now you're hurt but I'm giving fair warning that after you mend I'm going to take advantage of every situation that comes my way. For now, let's get this arm ready for a shower."

She looked at the top of his head and along his shoulders as he leaned over, positioning the bag and wrapping the tape. Blood still whipped through her veins at his words. He was mighty confident that she would be accepting his advances. Would she be able to fend them off? Did she want to?

"I'll leave you to your shower. Your clothes are on my bed. Call if you need anything. Meanwhile, I have a few phone calls to make."

She met his gaze. "Thanks. You really have gone the extra mile."

He shrugged. "Not a problem."

Maybe it wasn't a problem for him. Helping people seemed a part of who he was. She had to ponder that.

An hour later they were both dressed and ready to go. She'd had to ask him for help with her shirt and he'd been very professional, even averting his eyes a couple of times. They'd each had a quick bowl of cereal and Kiefer was now helping her settle into the passenger seat of his truck.

"I forgot one thing," he said as he stretched across her to belt her in.

Ashley looked at him in question.

"A good morning kiss."

His lips found hers. They were sure and tender. She couldn't resist pressing hers to his. Seconds later he pulled back, leaving her craving more of his touch. That had to stop. Anything extra might be detrimental to her heart. The life she planned.

Ashley's breaths were shorter than they should have been just from a simple kiss. What would it be like if he gave her a real one? Like their first one?

He circled the truck and climbed in.

Working to keep her tone light, she asked, "Is a morning kiss part of the ritual when a woman stays at your house?"

"Women don't come to my place." He started the truck.

Her heart flipped. She watched his profile as he backed out of the parking space. The man was starting to consume her life.

Kiefer twisted his coffee cup round and round on Ashley's table as he waited, not entirely patiently, for her to finish getting ready to go to the block party. When they had arrived at her place she'd gone full throttle. She'd started making calls, writing a list and hunting out clothes to wear. He worried that she was overdoing things but nothing he said was going to make her slow down. Ashley was in the zone. The best he could do was be there when pain overtook her or she wore out. At least he'd had the forethought to pick up food for them to take so she wouldn't be lifting pots and pans.

When he'd slid into bed beside her during the night he'd questioned the wisdom of doing so. The moment she'd snuggled up against him, all warm and sweet smelling, there had been no doubt he'd made a mistake. One that he would remember forever for both good and bad reasons. It had taken him too long to fall back to sleep with his body so painfully aware of hers. But he hadn't been able to act on that. She was hurt, needed comfort.

He'd watched her slowly wake up and had savored the moment she'd realized she'd been cuddled against him. There had been an appalled expression on her face before her gaze had fixed on his chest. Women had admired him before but never had one looked like she'd wanted to eat him up. His damaged ego had received such a boost of adrenaline he'd had to work at not grabbing Ashley and pulling her to him. If he had, she probably would have slapped him. She was the type of woman who needed to be finessed, romanced, unlike what he'd done when they'd first met.

When was the last time he'd romanced a woman? That had been his ex-wife and that hadn't turned out well. Romance wasn't what it was trumped up to be. Why did he feel compelled to do so now? Because of Ashley. For some reason she brought out the side of him he'd long ago squashed. He wanted to make her happy. Feel important.

Still, the honeyed way Ashley had returned his morning kiss had told him all he needed to know. She wasn't immune to his charms. She didn't need his romancing. All she needed was to make time for herself and her needs while she was trying to change the world.

A moan more of disgust than pain came from the direction of her room. He walked that way. "Is there a problem?"

"Yeah."

Kiefer stopped at her bedroom door. Ashley wore a light blue flowing dress with small straps. The color contrasted beautifully with her dark eyes and skin. She almost took his breath away.

"I hate this thing." She struggled to get the sling into place over her shoulder.

Grinning, he walked toward her. "Let me help." She turned her back to him. For once she didn't complain about his offer of assistance. He started untwisting the back strap, his fingers brushing her skin as he worked. Positioning the widest area of the strap over her shoulder, he stepped around her and adjusted it in the ring clasps. This time his fingers were too close to her tempting breasts. He'd lost his perspective as a physician and was thinking only as a man attracted to an alluring woman. Capturing Ashley's gaze, he asked, "How does that feel?"

She blinked at him a couple of times. Was he affecting her? Ashley was sure getting to him.

Stepping back, she said, "We need to get going. Did you get the folding chairs?"

"They're in the back of the truck."

"Good. The potato salad?"

How like her to deny what was happening between them. Keeping his face stoic, he answered, "I'll get it now. Do not go outside until I'm with you."

"Kiefer—"

"I mean it, Ashley."

"I won't. I'll wait for you."

Her ready agreement made him suspicious. She might not understand the danger, but he did. He hurried to get the potato salad from the refrigerator. Ashley stood by the front door. Together they exited, and all the while Kiefer kept scanning the area for anyone out of place.

"Do you really think someone would come after me in the middle of the day?"

"I don't know but we're not going to take any

chances. It doesn't hurt to be cautious." He led the way down the stairs.

"I'm sure I've not sounded like it but I am grateful for your help."

Kiefer glanced back, trying to gauge if she was being truthful. "Why the change of heart?"

"No change of heart. I was just thinking I might have been a little hard on you the last couple of days."

He steadied her when she faltered on the last step. "After all, what're friends for?"

She considered him a friend. That was unexpected and nice. Ashley would be a loyal friend, of that he had no doubt. Something that had been missing in his marriage.

# CHAPTER SIX

WHEN THEY ARRIVED at a park area near the river, Kiefer could tell it had been cleaned and groomed recently. Even the shrubbery had been trimmed. The large beach oaks surrounding the area provided shade from the already warm sun.

A few men were busy setting up tables. As they finished, a couple of women came behind them, rolling out plastic tablecloths.

Kiefer carried a large salad bowl. Ashley had requested he transfer the potato salad into one of hers. He placed it on a table already laden with food. He leaned the folding chairs he'd carried over his shoulder against a tree before he and Ashley joined some others.

As they approached, a heavyset woman wearing a bright smile stopped what she was doing and hurried toward them. "Ashley, are you okay, dear?"

"I'm fine. It's really just a scratch. The doctors…" she glanced at him "…just want me to be careful for a little while."

"Honey, you need to be more careful not to fall."

Kiefer looked at Ashley, who gave him a pleading look before she said, "I will. Mrs. Nasboom, I'd like you to meet the new doctor at the clinic, Dr. Bradford."

Mrs. Nasboom smiled up at him. "Nice to meet you, young man. I've heard a number of good things about you."

He smiled down at Mrs. Nasboom. "That's always good to hear."

"What do I need to do to help?" Ashley asked Mrs. Nasboom.

"I think we just need to set up the drinks table. We decided to put it over there." Mrs. Nasboom pointed toward a spot under one of the trees. There were already a couple of tables leaning against a large oak.

"We'll see to that," Ashley said.

When Mrs. Nasboom was out of earshot Kiefer looked Ashley straight in the eyes. "Fall?"

"Hush," she hissed, "or I'll tell them you pushed me." She walked away looking regal, like a queen.

*Ashley was something.*

As noon approached a crowd started gathering. Almost everyone made a point to come up and speak to Ashley. More than one had been a patient of his in the last few weeks. They often had something to say to him as well. Being an ER doctor, he rarely saw a patient twice. As the Southriver clinic doctor, he not only saw them more than once but had an opportunity to get to know something about his patients. He hadn't realized how much he had missed that connection until now.

Taking the clinic job had been his way of escaping. He'd needed to get away from Atlanta, from his past, and start over. The plan had turned out to have other benefits as well.

By noon the park was crowded with people talking and laughing. The tables almost groaned from the weight on them. The block party was achieving what Ashley had hoped for, a community coming together.

"Oh, honey, what happened to you?"

Kiefer turned from a conversation he was having with one of the local business owners to see an older woman dressed in a simple shirt and slacks hugging Ashley. When she released her, Kiefer could see Ashley favored her.

"Hi, Mom." Ashley looked at the balding man who reminded Kiefer of a banker standing behind her mother and said, "Hey, Dad. I'm glad you both could come."

"What're you talking about? We wouldn't have missed it," Ashley's mother said.

Her father gave her a hug and kissed her on the cheek. "Hi, sweetheart. What happened to you?"

Ashley seemed to hesitate. She didn't want to lie to her parents.

Kiefer walked over to them and said, "She took a tumble over the last step at her house. She'll be right as rain soon."

Her father studied him.

"I'm Kiefer Bradford, the clinic physician." He offered his hand to her father and they shook.

"You're the one Ashley has told us so much about." Ashley's mother beamed at him as if she knew something he didn't.

His attention went to Ashley, who was blushing. It was nice to see her a little less in control. "I hope it was good."

Her mother looked from one to the other. "Very

good. We've heard you're a wonderful doctor, not only from Ashley but from others too."

"Thank you for the compliment. I try to be."

"We were long overdue for medical help around here," Ashley's father said gruffly.

Kiefer met his look. "That's what I understand."

"Jean, Robert," someone called.

"We'll see you later, honey," her mother said to Ashley.

Mrs. Nasboom, still moving at the same speed as earlier, came up to them. "Ashley, we want you to say a few words before Pastor Marks says the blessing."

"Today isn't about me."

"No, but this was your idea. You need to say something," Mrs. Nasboom said as she turned to go.

"Okay, I'll be right there." Ashley adjusted her dress around her.

At least she hadn't been planning to use the event as a political stepping-stone, like so many politicians would have.

Ashley made her way through the crowd to a small group standing in front of them. Kiefer remained at the back. Ashley spoke to a man then turned to everyone and raised her hand. The crowd quieted. "Welcome, everyone. I'm so glad you came today."

Kiefer was impressed with the way she held the people spellbound. He'd always thought of himself as a people person but Ashley had real talent for commanding attention. She really was loved by the community. He could understand that. She was hard not to care about. But he wasn't going there.

"I hope this is the first of many community events that Southriver will host as we all work to make it a wonderful place to live. Before Pastor Marks blesses the food I'd like to introduce the new doctor at the clinic to anyone who hasn't already met him. Dr. Kiefer Bradford, wave your hand."

Kiefer did so and the people turned toward him and clapped enthusiastically. The man he assumed was Pastor Marks stepped up next to Ashley and offered a prayer. After that everyone lined up on both sides of the table and started filling their plates. Ashley was at the front of the line and he at the back. He spoke to those around him as he waited for his turn. They seemed like nice, honest people who were proud of their neighborhood. With his food in hand, he looked for Ashley. Normally he was uncomfortably aware of where she was. Now he felt lost without her, something he couldn't remember feeling with Brittney even after they were divorced.

A group of girls in their twenties stopped him. Between giggles they explained they were friends of Raeshell's, and he smiled at remembering his first patient's mother. Kiefer asked their names, which they offered with large smiles. They then talked about Raeshell and Mikey for a minute before he excused himself to find a place to eat lunch.

Seeing Ashley at one of the small picnic tables spaced around the area, he headed in her direction. He hadn't gone far when his name was called. It was Mrs. McGuire.

"Come join us, Doctor." She indicated an empty chair beside her.

Kiefer glanced at Ashley then walked over and joined the group sitting with Mrs. McGuire. Over the next hour or so he enjoyed hearing the stories of the group's childhoods and how much the community had changed. They all admired Ashley and supported her because of who she was and her work in their neighborhood.

He didn't even have to get up to get dessert. A woman took his empty food plate and thrust a large plate of cherry cobbler into his hands.

"Marsha Hardy makes the best cherry cobbler in Georgia. It isn't to be missed," Mrs. McGuire said.

It smelled heavenly. Kiefer put a forkful of the warm red mixture into his mouth. "Mmm."

"I told you so."

Kiefer covertly glanced around for Ashley.

"Looking for Ashley?" Mrs. McGuire was wearing a curious smile. "She's a good girl but I sometimes worry that she's too busy seeing about us and not herself. She needs a good man in her life. Children." Mrs. McGuire gave him a pointed look.

"We're just good friends." And they were, something he hadn't had with his ex. Still, something in him nudged him to want more.

The older woman harrumphed. "Yeah, I can tell that by the way you don't let her out of your sight."

"I just don't want her to get hurt again. She still has a sling on."

"You know, you're really not a good liar," Mrs. McGuire said flatly.

Kiefer hadn't felt this uncomfortable since he'd picked up the girl he'd asked to the prom. "I think I'll go see if there's any cobbler left."

Mrs. McGuire's chuckles followed him across the park.

Instead of returning to Mrs. McGuire, he walked toward Ashley, who was in a serious discussion with a group of men not far from the drinks table. As he approached she broke away and came toward him.

"I can tell you're starting to like it here, Dr. Bradford." She looked pointedly at his plate piled high with cobbler.

He grinned. "The ladies of Southriver can cook."

"Especially Ms. Hardy. I've not had a chance to have any."

"Too busy politicking." Kiefer filled a fork and offered it to her. "It's the best I've ever tasted."

Ashley leaned in and took the forkful. "It's wonderful."

Kiefer watched the movement of her lips as they slid over the fork. Even that simple action made blood rush to his groin. Did she make that same sound when she made love? He desperately wanted to find out.

"I'd like to show you something. Come this way."

He'd liked to show her a few things as well but they weren't thinking about the same things. Still, he was stunned she'd asked. This wasn't like her. "Sure."

He put his plate on a nearby table and they headed out of the park toward a block-long brick building across the road. At one time it had been a small factory. Now it was just a neglected structure fenced in, with grass growing around it. Beyond it was the Savannah River and the salt marshes.

"This is the building I was talking about the other day."

"The one with the view?" Kiefer studied the structure.

"Yep. I've never been inside but I've always thought it was a great old building. After seeing your place, I think it has promise. I'd love to have the entire top floor. Even have a roof garden."

"So why don't you look into buying it?"

"I can't afford it. I would need an investor, and being on the city council, I can't appear to have any conflicts of interest."

They continued walking along the fence.

Kiefer looked out at the slow-moving river. "You're right—it would have a great view."

"Families would even have a place for their kids to play across the street." Ashley turned toward the park.

Suddenly people were rushing out from under the trees away from the park.

Ashley stopped one of them. "What's going on?"

"A couple of guys are threatening people."

Ashley's heart thumped in her chest. The day had been going so well. They didn't need any trouble. Holding her arm, she hurried into the park. Kiefer followed. As they joined the people still there, she could see the drinks table had been turned over. Marko, along with two other members of his crew, was standing in front of everyone.

A couple of other men she didn't recognize stood to either side of the trio but were taking no aggressive action. They just watched carefully.

Ashley slowed her pace and walked up to Marko. She felt Kiefer close behind. She put on a bright smile. "Hi, Marko. We're so glad you could join us."

To his credit, the look on Marko's face was almost comical. He obviously hadn't anticipated that welcome.

"Would you like a plate to go? I missed seeing your mother. I'm sorry to hear she has been sick."

"We're not here for food," Marko growled.

"Then what're you here for?" Kiefer and the others took a step closer. She waved them back.

"We're seeing what you're doing."

"It's a neighborhood party. Anyone is welcome. You're part of the community, so you're welcome as long as you behave yourself." Ashley held her position.

"No one tells me what to do."

"Whether or not you stay or go is your business, but you're not going to destroy things like you did over there." She pointed toward the drinks table.

Marko stepped closer to her. Feet shifted around them.

Marko jerked his chin at her injured arm and smirked. "That hurt?"

"It did," Ashley said.

"If you don't stop, you'll get more than that," he snarled.

Kiefer stepped up beside her. Through clenched teeth he asked, "Are you saying you shot Ashley?"

She put her hand on Kiefer's arm. "Please don't start anything here. Now."

"That's right, Doc. Stay out of my way." Marko knocked over a food table as he stalked off. One of his buddies lifted another table and did the same. Everyone watched in disbelief as they left.

When Marko was out of sight the area erupted in chatter. The men started righting the tables and the women picked their dishes up off the ground.

"Everyone," Ashley called. "We've had a wonderful time here today. Please don't let a couple of mean people ruin it for us. We're a community of good people. That's what we need to remember." The tension in the crowd eased. "I hope to see you at the next get-together."

She was so glad her parents had already left and wasn't looking forward to their call about Marko. People continued to work at cleaning up but at a less frenzied pace. As she did her part where she could, Ashley noticed Kiefer talking to the men she hadn't recognized earlier. They shook hands and left before he joined her.

"Who were they?"

He hesitated a moment then said, "Just some friends of Bull's."

She glared at him. "I told you no police."

"They live in Southriver. I thought everyone was invited."

Ashley gave him a pointed look. "Did you ask them to come?"

"I asked Bull to see if he could have help here just in case something like what occurred happened. They were to hang back unless needed. That's just what they did."

As much as she would have liked to argue, he'd done the right thing.

Kiefer looked at her with concern. "How're you feeling? You have to be tired. If nothing else, of people asking about your arm."

Ashley was starting to fade. It had been a long day. "I'm fine. Let's finish here and go home."

For the next half hour they worked at cleaning up the park. Kiefer was beside her, doing what he could and assisting where she couldn't. Marko's appearance and show of temper had put a dampener on the day, no matter how hard she worked to put a positive spin on it.

Mrs. Nasboom stopped beside her. "It was a good day. We'll plan to do this or something like it in the fall. The committee won't let those thugs destroy what we're trying to do here."

"Thank you for saying that." Smiling gratefully, Ashley hugged her with her good arm.

"I have to ask you," Mrs. Nasboom said. "What really happened to your arm? I heard the doctor say something about you being shot?"

Ashley told her the truth and hoped that it wouldn't get out, but realistically it was inevitable. Hopefully it would be another couple of days before her parents heard.

The short return ride to Ashley's place was a quiet one. She was wearier than she wanted to admit. The block party had been going so well until Marko had shown up. She hadn't expected him, but glumly realized she should have. Maybe Kiefer was right. It was time for her to recognize the problems wouldn't be easily solved. That she was going to have to ask for police help.

"Kiefer."

"Huh?"

"I just want you to know I appreciate your help today. Especially you being concerned enough to see that we had police support in case things got out of hand. I didn't think Marko would be so bold."

His voice rose in disbelief. "After he shot you?"

"We don't know for sure it was him."

He gave her a look of disbelief. "Come on, Ashley. Either he did it or he had someone do it. He's dangerous. He's not that kid you used to know."

"I'm realizing that." She still couldn't tell him that she thought she had seen Marko in the parking lot. Didn't want to believe it.

Kiefer took her hand and squeezed it. "It was a good block party. You did a great job."

"You sure looked like you were having a good time when you were talking to those girls."

He grinned. "Were you jealous?"

"I was not!" Ashley pulled her hand away. She had been a little bit.

He pulled into the parking lot of her building.

"I think I'll take a nap." Ashley released her seat belt.

"I'll carry this bowl up for you and then I'm going down to the clinic and see if I can help out."

His friend was still filling in for him so he could go to the park with her.

Ashley wasn't sure how long she slept. Even though she was in her own bed, the rest hadn't been as sweet or deep as what she'd had in Kiefer's arms. She couldn't believe how quickly she'd come to depend on him for security. Her arm still ached but not like it had earlier. She moved it up and down, trying to judge her mobility.

Climbing out of bed, still wearing her sundress, she went to her kitchen for a glass of water. The door to the clinic stairs was open. Kiefer must have left it so in order to hear her. The man was very considerate. Muffled voices came from below. He was still seeing patients. Returning to her living room, she settled into her favorite chair and turned on the TV. Finding a romance movie, she tried to get involved in it but all she could think about was Kiefer. She missed him. He'd become an everyday and sometimes nighttime fixture in her life. How had he managed to weave himself into her life so completely?

Footfalls in her hallway made her back tense. Was it Marko again? She had to get beyond that. She'd felt fear enough as a child.

"Are you watching that channel that hates men?" It was nice to hear Kiefer's deep voice.

She smiled. "They don't hate men. It just looks like they do."

"I'm getting ready to head home. I just wanted to make sure you don't need help with anything and to make sure you lock up. A couple of security guys will be around here all night."

"Do you have to go right now?"

He blinked. "Not really."

"I'd like some company. How about watching a movie?"

Kiefer nodded. "Okay, but no chick flicks."

Ashley giggled. "Fair enough. All my movies are in that drawer." She pointed under the TV. "While you decide on one I'll fix some popcorn."

She made her way to the kitchen. What had got into her? What was she thinking, inviting the most attractive male she knew to spend the evening with her? Aggressive in almost every part of her life, asking a man to spend time with her was out of character. She was opening a box she might not be able to close again. Even if she wanted to.

Kiefer was sitting on the sofa with his shoes lying on the floor and his feet propped up on the coffee table when she returned. He looked relaxed, as if he belonged. She placed the bowl of popcorn on the table and took a seat beside him, but not too close.

"What did you decide on?"

"*Star Wars*. The original." He pushed a button on the remote and the movie started.

"Good choice."

She picked up the bowl and offered it to him.

He took a handful. "I ate so much today I don't know if I can eat any more."

"I know what you mean." She placed the bowl on the table again and sat back against the sofa.

Kiefer put his free hand around her waist and gently pulled her over next to him. His arm came to rest on the sofa above her shoulders. "That's better."

It was. A lot better. She laid her head on his shoulder. That was even nicer. Kiefer's heart beat at a steady rhythm beneath her ear.

They were about half an hour into the movie when Kiefer whispered, "Ashley."

She looked at him. His mouth found hers. The smell and taste of salted popcorn filled her head. He pulled back slightly then brushed his lips across hers before settling firmly on them. Her toes curled and her fingers itched to cling to him. Warmth permeated her inside, melted her resistance. Desire flared. She couldn't remember the last time a man had been as sexually attentive as Kiefer. Or made her feel more.

Too quickly he pulled away. "I've wanted to do that all day and I just couldn't wait any longer."

Ashley put her good arm around his neck and tugged his mouth down to hers again. She wanted more, needed everything from him. During the last few days things had changed between them. She'd come to depend on him. He had to know she wanted him, craved him. Pressing closer, she ran her hand through his hair. His tongue teased the seam of her lips and she opened for him.

She found heaven. A warm paradise. A place of security. Her tongue joined his in a dance that made her center throb. She grazed the back of his neck with her nails as he lowered her to the sofa. With his lips never leaving hers, he shifted to cover her body.

When he touched her hurt arm she flinched. He paused. She shushed him and pulled him back to her. Her whole body quaked with desire. She wanted him. Now.

Kiefer's mouth skimmed her cheek. She moaned. He breathed, "I don't want to hurt you."

"I don't care." Ashley directed his mouth back to hers, pouring all her passion into the kiss. She flexed her hips against him.

He broke away. Kissed her temple. "If you keep that up, this might be the fastest lovemaking session ever."

"I want you."

He rose up enough that he could look down at her. "In this you aren't in charge. We're partners."

She met his gaze. "Whatever you say."

"That's more like it. First off, and I can't believe I'm asking this, is this what you want? I'll accept no regrets in the morning."

Ashley nodded agreement as she fumbled with a button on his shirt and slid a finger through the opening to touch his skin. "Very sure."

"Are you feeling up to this? I wouldn't hurt you for the world."

She lifted up so that she could kiss the side of his mouth. "Why, Dr. Bradford, are you trying to talk me into or out of bed?"

"I've been thinking about this for days and don't want to mess it up."

How like him to be concerned for her. "Then why don't you shut up and kiss me?"

He cupped each side of her face, sliding his fingers into her hair, and brought his mouth to hers. The kiss was powerful, going straight to her soul. Kiefer had some type of power over her. This was more like it. She sighed. Her hand kneaded his shoulder while the fingers of the hand in the sling brushed along his ribs.

His mouth moved over her lips, begging and giving at the same time. He shifted and pressed against her arm. She squeaked with pain.

He was off her in a flash. Oaths were said low and sharp.

She stood and took his hand. "I'm fine. Let's find somewhere more comfortable."

Ashley tugged him toward her bedroom. She paused halfway there, turned to give him a kiss. To her pleasure he groaned. She flicked her tongue over his lips. Without warning, he took control, turning it hot and wet. A growl rolled from deep within his throat as he wrapped his arms around her. Her feet came off the floor. Kiefer carried her into the bedroom. At the bed, he let her slide down his body. "I'm going to do what I wanted to do the other night. Undress you."

He slowly removed the sling from her arm then brushed a kiss over her lips. His hands came to her shoulders and skimmed her flimsy dress straps down her arms. He placed a kiss on the ridge of her shoulder. Briefly he fingered her necklace.

Ashley shivered. Could she stand this much attention until he was done?

"Turn around." His hands went to her waist and gently guided her so her back was to him. His lips flicked over the skin just below her neck. She shook.

"Like that, did you?" He didn't wait for an answer as he stroked his fingers at the top of her dress where the zipper started. Slowly, almost painfully so, he opened the closure until her dress hung by the straps at her elbows. His large, warm hands traveled along her rib cage until his fingers cupped her breasts still secure in her strapless bra.

"Perfect," he murmured in her ear, before he placed a kiss below her earlobe.

His hands began to work magic, making her breasts tingle and her nipples harden. Stepping closer, Kiefer pressed his ridged manhood against the small of her back. As one of his hands continued to lift and test her breasts, the other skimmed along her body, pushing her dress over her hips until it fell to the floor. One of his palms settled over her belly and pulled her back against him. She moaned.

Kiefer's hand left her and seconds later her bra fell away. Ashley shivered as the cool air of the room touched her sensitive breasts. That same hand returned to twirl a nipple between two fingers, making her womb contract. She leaned her head back against his chest, her breathing turning to short gasps.

Teeth nibbled at the top of her shoulder before his lips journeyed up her neck. "Sweet. So sweet," he murmured, as he took her earlobe between his teeth. "I'm hungry for you."

His hand at her breasts captured her other one, his fingers circling that nipple. Kiefer's other hand moved farther along her skin until he found the top of her panties. His fingers traced the distance of the lace at the top then back again before they slipped beneath.

Ashley sucked in a breath. Held it. Waited. Wanted.

His fingers tormented her breast. Warm, wet kisses found the spot behind her ear. The tip of his tongue flicked out to taste her skin. Kiefer's hand moved lower, brushing curls. "Share with me."

She widened her stance. He sucked gently on the curve of her neck as his hand cupped her heat. A finger found her core. Slipped in. Exited, to return.

Her panting was the only sound in the room. Blood roared in her ears. Kiefer's hand left her center and his thumb hooked in her panties, pulling them down. They rolled along her thighs and he shoved them to her knees. From there they fell and she stepped out of them. His hand glided up her leg, across her thigh to cup her again.

Kiefer's finger entered and left her core as his other hand rhythmically massaged her breasts in turn while his mouth kissed and nipped over her skin. She was on fire, the throbbing becoming a drumming. Urgency tightened in her, twisting and swirling, squeezing until she squirmed against him. Ridged with tension, she was being driven to begging, gasping for release. Yet Kiefer continued his assault.

Another thrust of his finger and she closed her eyes, pushed against him and keened her pleasure before becoming weak in his arms. Her knees buckled. Kiefer's soft, satisfied chuckle brushed her ear as he held her close.

Turning her around, he pulled her tightly against him and gave her an openmouthed kiss that only made her desire more of his attention. She'd never imagined foreplay could be so powerful. Or perfect.

"This time I want to watch you." Kiefer breathed as he looked into Ashley's flushed face. She was so beautiful. He lifted her to the bed.

"Unfair. You have your clothes on," she teased.

"That's easily remedied." His eyes locked with hers as he jerked his shirt over his head. She watched him unbuckle his belt and release it. He pulled a packet from his wallet before pushing his pants and underwear over his hips. They fell to the floor. He stepped out of them. With perverse pride he watched as Ashley's eyes widened as she gazed at his manhood. When her lips curved into a small smile, his heart beat hard against his ribs. She liked what she saw. His chest swelled. With her he wasn't lacking, like he had been with Brittney. Ashley had a way of making him feel like a man among men. Kiefer was tempted to thump his chest.

"Come here," Ashley all but purred, as she pushed back on the bed.

Maybe where lovemaking was concerned, having a self-confident woman in bed could have its advantages. He opened the foil package and covered himself.

"I don't have to be asked twice." Kiefer came down between her legs and moved over her to place his hands on either side of her head. His mouth found hers. She was waiting, warm and wet, to welcome him. Ashley wrapped her good arm around his waist. He was careful not to apply any pressure to her other one. Shifting, his length nudged her opening.

His arms trembled with the effort not to slam into her. He wanted her so badly. But she deserved care, tenderness. Ashley broke the kiss and looked at him. Pushing forward, he found her opening and stopped. Her gaze still held his. She lifted her hips in invitation. With a thrust he filled her. She smiled and pulled his lips down for a kiss.

Mouths locked, Kiefer pulled back and moved forward, setting a rhythm that Ashley joined. Had he found heaven? He thrust again and Ashley's eyes widened. Her mouth formed an O before she tensed and pushed her hips upward. He watched as a look of wonder filled her eyes, a brush of amazement eased her features and she came apart before him.

With one more shove of his hips Kiefer joined her in the joy of suspended satisfaction.

# CHAPTER SEVEN

ASHLEY WOKE CURLED against Kiefer's side, with her injured arm resting on his chest. It felt right, safe, being there. Her lips found skin.

In a raspy, low voice he murmured, "Mmm."

She'd had the best night of her life. Too good. It made her want more. But was that possible?

Kiefer's hand followed the curve of her hip and returned to cup a breast. "Good mornin'."

He sounded so sexy. So much so that she wanted to hang on to him forever. But that wasn't the way things worked in Southriver. He was a transient person and would be gone when his time was done. But until he left she planned to enjoy the time she had. Make the most of having him around. Was it selfish? Yes. But for once she was going to do something for herself. She'd deal with the fallout when the time came.

She kissed his chest again.

"I'd stop that unless you plan to back it up with something more."

"Oh, I have every intention of backing it up. Can you handle it?"

"You just take your best shot."

Ashley rolled, came up on her knees and straddled him. His manhood was already standing at full attention. She leaned forward with the intention of claiming his mouth.

He stopped her with a hand to her shoulder. "How's your arm?"

"You let me worry about that. You need to be concerned about whether or not you can stand up to what's coming your way."

He gave a throaty chuckle. "Bring it on, Alderman."

She caressed him with her tongue as she lifted her hips and slowly slid down his shaft.

Sometime later Ashley noticed that the sun streaming through the bathroom window came from high in the sky. She was enjoying Kiefer running his fingers through her hair as he shampooed it. She'd found a number of ways she liked being taken care of. "I would like to try this in your shower sometime. It's a little roomier."

"You're welcome anytime. But I rather like the closeness of yours." He rubbed his wet body against hers as he reached for the conditioner.

When she turned, licked a rivulet of water from the skin over his heart, Kiefer pinned her against the side of the shower, his intention clear in his eyes and in his body.

Ashley laughed. She'd done that more with Kiefer than with anyone else in her life and she liked it. For those seconds she forgot about the pain there could be in life. "Hey, what about my arm?"

He backed away. "Now you're going to use that as an excuse?"

"It worked, didn't it?" she said as she stepped out of the tub and grabbed a towel.

"I think you're teasing me." Kiefer joined her on the bath mat.

She grinned up at him. "Every chance I can get."

He reached over and lifted the stone that hung on her necklace. "You wear this all the time. What is it about?"

She took it from him. "Lizzy gave it to me. The day she died."

"You've worn it every day since?"

She nodded.

"You want to make sure you remember."

Kiefer understood. "I don't want to forget. It's too easy to forget."

He kissed her forehead then took her towel from her and started drying her off. A few seconds later he said, "Hey, it's Sunday. Why don't we go over to Tybee and spend the day?"

When was the last time she'd just taken a day for herself? Not thought about the next council meeting? Had to meet with someone? She looked at Kiefer, tall and naked in front of her. "I'd like that."

"Great. You put on your tiniest bathing suit so I can admire your beautiful body, and pack a bag, and we'll go to my place on the way for my suit."

He was like a kid happy to play for the day and it was rubbing off on her.

An hour later they were driving over the short causeway to Tybee Island. The sun was shining brightly as Kiefer pulled his truck into the last open parking spot in the lot next to the Tybee Island lighthouse. Together they carried their bags and beach chairs toward the water.

He picked a space away from the crowd but near enough to the water for Ashley to enjoy the sound of waves lapping, then opened and set the chairs next to each other.

His low whistle of admiration when she removed her shirt and shorts made Ashley blush. She savored knowing that he liked her body. He'd certainly shown it last night. "I'm going to lie on a towel for a while. Maybe take a nap." Ashley adjusted her towel on the sand.

He grinned. "Didn't sleep much last night?"

"No, but I did enjoy myself."

Kiefer took the chair closest to her. "That was the plan. Turn your back to me and let me put some sunscreen on you. I don't want you to burn."

She did as he asked and relished the feel of his strong hands applying the lotion. He'd changed her in a significant way. This care she could get used to. Lying down, she was soon asleep.

"Hey, sleepyhead. Let's go swimming." Kiefer was using the point of an inflatable raft to tickle her back.

Ashley rolled over and offered him her hand. He took it and pulled her to a standing position beside him. "There's no rest for the weary around you," she grumbled.

"I'm not that bad, am I?" He sounded concerned, raft tucked under his arm.

She caught his hand and pulled him toward the water. "I'm just kidding."

As they entered the water Kiefer pulled back. "I brought this float so you could rest your arm on it. That way, maybe you won't get it too wet."

He really was thoughtful. How could his ex-wife have ever wanted more than what he could give? "You think of everything. The salt water will be good for it."

"Yes, but you still need to keep it as dry as possible."

Ashley splashed him. "Wasn't the beach your idea?"

"Yeah. It might not have been my best. I forgot about your arm."

"Why, Doctor, where was your mind?"

Kiefer wrapped an arm around her waist and pulled her to him. "I was thinking about you, just not your arm." His lips found hers. Abruptly releasing her, he dived under, coming up again farther out in deeper water.

She floated as she watched him make strong, sure strokes through the ocean. After a while his head went under, to reappear near her. He took the other end of the float.

She played in the water as she asked, "I've been meaning to ask you—where did you get the name Kiefer?"

"From my parents."

She splashed him. "You know what I mean. It's such an unusual name."

He grinned. "My mother and my aunt Georgina had this big crush on a movie star who had the name. They both said they were going to name their sons after him. My uncle said his child would be named after him. So I got the name."

"Your father didn't mind?"

"No, he was just happy to have a son. Mother could have named me anything she wanted."

"Do you have brothers and sisters?" Ashley enjoyed dabbling her hand in the sway of the waves.

"Yeah. A brother—he and his family live in Atlanta—and a sister. She lives in Jacksonville, Florida. How about you?"

"One brother. He's in the service. We don't see much of him, but the internet and cell phones are great things." Richey would like Kiefer.

"You miss him?"

"I do. He was sort of my buffer between me and my daddy."

"How's that?" Kiefer pushed his wet hair back off his forehead.

"As long as I was with him, my parents would let me go places. He became my ticket out into the world."

"I know what happened with your friend was tough but were your parents really that overprotective?"

She nodded. "They were. It destroyed our family's friendship with the family next door. My parents questioned why they hadn't seen the ugliness in Ron. They feared what he might have done to us. They started second-guessing every decision they made until it was easier just to have us stay home than it was to take a chance on something happening to us."

His face turned serious. "I know something about that second-guessing."

She watched him, waiting for him to say more. Finally he did but it came out harsh and painful.

"You know I mentioned my mother was attacked?" She nodded and he continued. "She brought a homeless man home for a meal. What he wanted was money for drugs, not food. I watched him beat my mother for her purse and did nothing. I should have done something. At least your parents tried to protect you."

Ashley studied him closely. Pain filled her for the kid who had seen such brutality. They had more in common than she'd first thought. "How old were you when that happened?"

"Seven."

"You were just a kid! What did you expect you could do?"

"Instead of hiding in the laundry closet, I could have hit him or something. Anything. Screamed." The disgust with himself filled his voice. Did he really carry this around all the time? Why wouldn't he? She always carried the pain of Lizzy.

"And been hurt yourself?"

"That doesn't ease the guilt."

Ashley was well aware of what selfishness did to a person. All these many years later she still felt responsible for refusing to walk home with Lizzy that day. It might have made the difference. She hadn't wanted to get her fancy new boots muddy, walking across an empty lot, so she'd said no, despite Lizzy's begging.

Rubbing her hand up and down Kiefer's arm, Ashley said, "I'm sure your mother doesn't blame you. Did they catch him?"

"Yes. I had to give a description of the guy because Mother was in the hospital. When the reporters and TV found out a kid had seen it all, they were everywhere."

"That's why you didn't care anything about being on camera when the TV crew was at the clinic."

"Yeah, I've had enough of that to last a lifetime." A wave bumped their bodies against each other. "Enough of that depressing talk. I'd rather be touching you."

He let go of the raft, leaving Ashley to hold it. Standing, with the salt water at chest level, Kiefer faced her and placed his hands under her arms. Slowly he followed the path of her curves down to her hips. Cupping her butt, he squeezed then brought her to him for a kiss.

A wave washed over them, ripping them apart. Laughing and spluttering when they came up, they saw the float being carried away.

"I think you need to go dry off your arm," Kiefer said. "I'll get the float and be in in a minute."

"You're not coming with me?"

"This is a family beach, and if I come out of the water right now, after that kiss, I'd be an X-rated view."

Ashley laughed. "Need a cold shower, do you, Doc?"

He started toward her. "Maybe the alderman wants to be on the front page of the newspaper for swimming topless."

Ashley shrieked and hurried for the beach.

"That'll teach you to make fun of me!" Kiefer called, as she walked up the sand toward their chairs.

Kiefer saw the grin spread across Ashley's face when he joined her. This time she had taken a chair next to his.

"Feeling better?" she cooed.

He put the float down and dropped into his chair. "Yes, no thanks to you."

The view of her backside as she'd walked up the beach hadn't eased his pain. His feelings were too sharp and intense for his peace of mind. What he had worked so hard to prevent had happened. He cared about Ashley.

They had been drying off in the sun for a few minutes when she asked, "Can we walk over and see the lighthouse?"

"Sure, why not."

Ashley pulled on her T-shirt and shorts over her bathing suit. Kiefer didn't bother with a shirt. They both slipped their feet into flip-flops. Hand in hand they walked toward the tall brick tower painted black with a white band three-quarters of the way up.

"I've always loved lighthouses." She sighed. "There's something romantic about them."

Kiefer stopped and looked at her. "And the surprises keep coming. First romance movies. Now lighthouses. What could be next?"

"I'll give you a real shock. I read romance novels."

His mouth gapped in exaggerated shock. "Are you learning anything in those books I could benefit from?"

She swatted his arm. "Maybe."

"I look forward to finding out."

They walked along the road a distance across a grassy area to the white picket fence entrance then toward the red-roofed house that was attached to the light tower. Beside it was a large white event tent. White netting had been tied in bows on the chairs and netting draped to create an altar.

"Look." She smiled broadly. "They're getting ready for a wedding. This is a beautiful place for one."

"Every woman likes a wedding," he said, more to himself than her. His ex had. That apparently was the only thing she'd liked about being married to him. Except for the best man. Neither weddings nor marriage interested him but he had no doubt they did Ashley. It was a gulf he wasn't sure they could cross.

"And how like a man to be cynical about them."

"I have good reason."

They walked around the outside of the lighthouse. "I've always wondered what it would be like to live in a house like this, with the water surrounding you. Listening to the rush of the waves during a storm and knowing that the light above was the difference between a sailor's life or death."

"You really are a romantic. I've always wondered how the light-keeper walked all those steps every day."

Ashley laughed. "We do see things from two different perspectives."

He pulled her close for a quick hug. "Yeah, but we see eye to eye on a few things."

They spent an hour looking through the museum and talking about the life of a caretaker.

"Well, are you ready for it?" Kiefer asked.

"For what?"

"To climb to the top." He opened the door to the spiral staircase.

"If you can, I can." Ashley gave him a determined look. He admired how she approached everything with a can-do spirit.

"Okay, but don't overwork that arm just to try to outdo me."

"Eat my dust." Ashley took the lead and she started up the stairs.

They climbed and circled, stopping a couple of times to catch their breath before they stepped into the lamp room.

"Oh, my, you can see forever," Ashley said in wonder.

"You've never been up here?"

"No, our family didn't journey far. With the business to run, there wasn't much time to do anything else."

Kiefer contemplated how very different their family lives had been. "And you've not been out here since leaving home?"

She continued to stare out at the ocean. "You know how it is. We don't visit the places closest to us." With a sigh she turned away from the view. "They sure have done a great job of preserving this place. I wish someone with money would take a real interest in Southriver."

"Always a crusader."

"What's wrong with wanting to make things better?"

Kiefer opened the door to the catwalk and she preceded him. "Nothing, unless it consumes your life until you don't have time for anything else."

Ashley turned to look at him. "I'm taking time today."

"Yeah, but when was the last time you did?"

She stood thinking.

"Exactly."

"I'm doing something important," Ashley threw over her shoulder as they walked around the top of the tower.

"Agreed. But what're your plans once you get Southriver into shape?"

"I don't know. There's always another area of the city that can be improved. Who knows, I might run for senator and work on the state."

There was what he'd been expecting. It wasn't all about Southriver. She was thinking of her future as well. "So you never plan to get married or have children?"

She gave him a speculative look, brows raised. "Why? You asking?"

"That was a general question, not one in particular. I've gone down the marriage route and it didn't work out."

"So you're done with it?"

They started down the stairs. "Apparently I'm not any good at it."

"Maybe you didn't have the right partner," Ashley offered.

Ahead of her, Kiefer muttered, "Learning to

trust again is a tough thing to do." Something he wasn't sure he could ever do again.

She nodded, understanding more than anyone. "Yes, it is."

Two afternoons later Ashley was at home when her cell phone rang. She was surprised to see on the ID that it was Kiefer, who she'd seen downstairs only a half an hour earlier. Why would he be calling? He could just come up.

"Hey, what's up?" she answered.

"I thought you might like to know that your mother is here."

"What's happened?" Panic filled her.

Kiefer said in a calm voice, "She had a small kitchen accident. She'll be fine."

"I'll be right down."

As Ashley came out of the stairwell she saw Margaret in the hall. She pointed to an exam room and Ashley headed that way. Giving the door a quick knock, she entered the room. Her mother was sitting on the exam table with Kiefer on a stool beside it, holding her hand.

Ashley rushed to them. "Mother, what have you done?"

Her mother's eyes held pain. "I was pouring boiling pasta water into the colander and spilled it on my hand. Stupid mistake. And painful."

Ashley studied the angry red skin over the top of her mother's hand that Kiefer held.

"I'm going to need to clean and bandage this. If you don't take care of it you'll be vulnerable to infection," Kiefer said as he pushed the stool back and stood. "I'll be right back."

"Mom, where is Dad?"

"At the store."

"You drove yourself here? You should have called me." Ashley pulled the chair out of the corner.

"Like you called us when you were shot?" Her mother's voice was accusing yet laced with concern.

"I was fine. I didn't want you to worry. I was in good hands. Kiefer was right there to take care of me."

"And he lied to us."

"Please don't blame him. I asked him not to say anything. Made him promise—and he's a doctor, so it's patient confidentiality. I know I should have told you but I couldn't believe it at first."

"Ashley, we're your parents. We're going to worry. And we deserved to know, not hear it from someone who came into the store."

Ashley hadn't thought about that happening. She'd been so caught up in her own inability to accept that someone would do such a thing.

"You should have told us."

"You're right. It won't happen again. You deserve to be treated better." Ashley pointed her finger at her mother. "But it works both ways."

Kiefer entered, carrying a handful of supplies and a plastic bottle under one arm. He set a metal pan and a couple of bandage boxes on the exam table beside her mother, then the bottle. Looking at Ashley, he said, "Margaret is seeing to another patient. Do you mind helping me a sec?"

Ashley had no nursing experience but she would do what she could. "Sure."

He handed her the pan. "I'm going to pour the saline solution over your mother's hand and I just need you to hold the pan below it."

"I can do that."

"Mrs. Marsh, this will sting a little but I assure you it's necessary."

"Can I believe you?"

"Uh?" Kiefer gave her mother a perplexed look.

"You've lied to me before." Her mother glared at Kiefer.

"Mother!" Ashley barked.

He glanced at Ashley then looked back at her mother. "I promise never to mislead you again."

Her mother nodded. "I expect to hold you to that. Now, let's get on with this."

Kiefer appeared relieved to no longer be under her mother's scrutiny. He opened the top to the bottle and handed the pan to Ashley. Kiefer carefully took her mother's hand and held it over the pan. Slowly he poured the saline over the tender area until the container was empty. Using a gauze square, he cautiously patted the area dry.

The man was amazingly gentle. That was a rare quality in any person. He'd proved to have a number of positive attributes.

"I'm done with the pan," he said, and Ashley placed it on a nearby stand. "Mrs. Marsh, I would like you to hold it up like this." Bending her arm at the elbow so that it was at a ninety-degree angle, Kiefer opened and applied a tube's worth of salve to the damaged area. With that done, he wrapped gauze over it and neatly applied a purple elastic bandage.

By the time he was done, her mother was biting her lower lip. Kiefer stood and patted her on the shoulder. "Take an over-the-counter pain reliever and keep it dry. Let me see you again in a week. Call me if there is a problem."

"Thank you. You really are as good as they say you are," Jean said.

Kiefer smiled. "I consider that a high compliment, coming from you. Thank you."

Ashley took her mother's uninjured arm and helped her from the table. "Come on, Mother. I'll take you home."

As they passed Kiefer, Ashley reached out and grabbed his hand for a second and caught his gaze. He was one of the good guys. Someone who truly cared about people. A man she could trust. She mouthed, "Thank you."

The next week went by, with Kiefer waking up to Ashley nestled against him or her arm wrapped around his waist and her body spooned against his back. There was contentment in this arrangement he didn't wish to examine. More often than not, they showered together in the morning, a ritual he was enjoying too much. They spent their time at both of their places depending on where Ashley's schedule took her. Despite doctor's orders, she insisted that she would have no problem driving. She would do what she pleased, no matter what he said.

Her strong personality, independence and genuine love of people were what he liked best about her, but they were also the traits that made him worry. She went headlong and heart open into everything she did. If she wasn't more cautious she would be in serious trouble one day, but for now he was there for her.

As far as he was concerned, life was good. There had been no more incidents around the clinic, and according to Bull, there was no evidence strong enough to arrest Marko for shooting at Ashley. Kiefer still kept a cautious eye out for anyone or anything unusual. A security man watched the clinic at night, which added some comfort.

Thursday afternoon, Kiefer was coming out of an examination room when he saw his mother sitting in the waiting room. "Mom, what're you doing here?"

"I have some supplies and I thought I'd just deliver them."

Kiefer kissed her. "I wish you had called first. I could have got them from you."

"I wanted to see the place."

"This isn't a part of town you need to be in by yourself."

She put her hand on his cheek. "Honey, I'll be fine."

That was exactly what she'd said the day she'd lain bloody and bruised on the floor of their kitchen. She sounded so much like Ashley.

"How about telling me where to unload the supplies and then show me around." His mother's suggestion dispelled the dark memories.

"I can do that." Ashley's voice came from behind him.

Kiefer gave her a huge smile, always glad to see her even if they'd only been apart a few minutes. "Hi."

"Hey."

He wanted to give Ashley a kiss but they had agreed not to make their relationship public because of her position on the city council. They didn't want to give the media a news story. Plus they just wanted their personal lives to remain private.

Kiefer turned back to his mother, who was grinning and watching them closely. They weren't covering very well. He cleared his throat. "Mom, I think you know Ashley Marsh."

"Yes. We have met a number of times. Hi, Ashley."

"Hello, Mrs. Bradford. It's nice to see you again."

"Please make it Maggie," his mother said.

"Maggie it is. Why don't you show me those supplies and we'll get them in?"

Both women ignored him as they walked down the hall toward the waiting room. Kiefer smiled. Two peas in a pod.

Sometime later he heard talking in his office, which doubled as a storeroom. Ashley and his mother, both wearing business dress and not letting it matter, worked side by side as they unloaded boxes. They were deep in a conversation that he wasn't going to interrupt and hoped wasn't about him. He wasn't sure how he felt about the two most important women in his life spending so much time together. Coming to an abrupt halt, he focused on his realization. That was what Ashley had become to him—important. He'd stepped over the line and wasn't sure if he could step back or even wanted to.

Some hours later Kiefer had seen his last patient and was locking up the clinic behind Margaret when he realized his mother hadn't said goodbye before leaving. That was unlike her. He must have been so busy that she hadn't wanted to bother him. Flipping off the hall lights, he climbed the back stairs to Ashley's place. He tensed at the sound of voices. Ashley should be by herself. Was Marko making a move again?

He slowly stepped back down the stairs and picked up the baseball bat he'd bought and placed inside the stairwell for just such an occasion. Picking it up, he crept up the stairs again. With the bat raised in his hand, he slowly pushed the door open.

His mother and Ashley looked up from what they were doing at the table, saw the bat and stared at him as if he had gone crazy.

He looked at his mother. "I thought you had left."

His mother looked puzzled. "No, not yet. Why're you carrying a bat?"

"I didn't know someone was with Ashley."

"You visit her with a bat in hand all the time?" His mother turned in her chair to face him, concerned.

"Only when I'm worried she might be attacked."

"Why would you be concerned about that?" his mother asked.

Ashley took the bat from him. She placed it on the first step of the stairs. "Because someone I know came in unexpectedly the other week."

"And she was shot at!" Kiefer couldn't help but say.

"What?" Maggie's alarmed gaze met his.

"I'm fine. Nothing to worry about." As usual, Ashley played down the problem.

That might be the way she saw it, but he didn't.

His mother stood. "It's time for me to go anyway. Ashley, thank you for an interesting afternoon. It was nice to get to know you better. I look forward to working with you on our fund-raiser."

So his mother and Ashley had been up here, hatching some plan.

"I am too. Thanks for all the supplies. I promise they'll be put to good use."

"I'm confident they will be. Kiefer, why don't you walk me out to my car?"

Ashley led the way to her front door. Kiefer followed his mother out. He checked the area as they walked toward her car. He nodded at the security guard standing near the front corner of the building.

"She's a smart girl, Kiefer." His mother patted his arm. "Try not to worry so."

"Ashley's like you. She takes chances that she shouldn't."

"You can only do what you can do. I know you feel guilty that you didn't do anything when I was beaten. But you aren't the one who should feel that way. I'm the one who should carry that burden. I had no business bringing home that man. I overstepped. I put you in danger."

"Mom—"

"No, you hear me out. No child should witness that. It created a vein of distrust in you. I watched you become wary of people. When you finally did let someone in, of all things, she made you distrust more. I'm sorry for that. But not all people are bad. You must remember that. Have a little faith in Ashley and ease up on yourself." His mother settled behind the wheel of her car. "You deserve to be happy. Give yourself a chance."

"We're just friends, Mom."

His mother smiled. "Friends don't look at each other the way you two did in the hall today."

"Just don't build it up into something it isn't."

She patted his hand, which was resting on the door window. "And you should recognize when you have someone worth fighting for."

Kiefer returned to Ashley's apartment to find her in the kitchen, cooking supper. "I'm sorry if I overreacted."

She turned to him. "I understand. Really, I do."

"I hear a 'but' in there."

"Yeah. You're going to have to learn to control your protective instinct." Ashley turned the stove off and came to him, wrapping her arms around his waist.

"I can make no promises." He pulled her into a hug.

"I'm not asking for any. Just asking you to try."

"That I can do."

She kissed his chin. "I think your mother knows there's something going on between us."

"I think she does too." He grinned. "You made

it pretty obvious that you were glad to see me this afternoon."

"Me? You're the one who looked happy to see me."

Kiefer squeezed her butt. "I was. I am now." He kissed her deeply, walking her back against the wall. His mouth went to her neck. "Almost as sweet as Marsha Hardy's cherry cobbler."

"What about supper?" Ashley asked.

He started removing her clothes. "I'm interested in dessert."

# CHAPTER EIGHT

A WEEK LATER Kiefer was dressing for the day when Ashley said, "I'll be late tonight. I've got a council subcommittee meeting until ten."

"I'll pick you up."

"Kiefer, I understand your concern for me. I truly do, but you can't watch over me 24-7. I don't want it and you have a job to do. I'll be fine."

"I'm sure you will be but I'd like to do it anyway."

"I've been taking care of myself for years. I'm not going back to the way it was when I was a kid. Lighten up."

Wasn't that what his mother had told him? "Okay. I'll see you at my place?"

"No, back here. I have an early meeting with local businesspeople tomorrow."

He would feel better about her coming to his place but didn't push it.

Kiefer saw nothing of Ashley during the day.

He kept an eye out for her car but it was never in the parking lot. His day was busy and apparently hers was as well. After closing the clinic, he climbed the stairs to her place. He missed the noise and smell of Ashley cooking their dinner, and more than that her waiting with a smile. He had it bad. Worse than ever. To have been so determined to just have a good time and not get attached, he'd failed miserably. He'd fallen in love with the one woman who could drive him crazy emotionally and physically.

In love! After Brittney he'd sworn never to go there again. But he was completely absorbed with Ashley.

Time clicked slowly by as he waited for her to return. Having alerted the night security man that Ashley would be coming in late, he watched the evening shows, listening for a car. When the nightly news started and it was half an hour past time for Ashley to come home, he called her. Her phone went to voice mail.

Kiefer paced the floor, stopping long enough to look out the window, hoping to see car headlights. Taking a shower, he tried to convince himself that when he'd finished Ashley would be there. She wasn't. He'd left his cell phone on the bathroom counter in case she called. Before he dried off, he checked to see if she had. No luck.

Still searching for light crossing the windows signaling Ashley's return, fear became a tighter knot in his chest. His imagination had him seeing Marko and his gang driving Ashley off the road. After an hour and a half the sound of a car door closing told him Ashley was home. He waited on the landing of her front door when she started up the stairs.

"I expected you ages ago. Where have you been?" he demanded, hands balled tight at his sides.

Even in the dim light he saw her body language change, stiffen. Become defensive. "We were in a deep discussion and a couple of us went out for coffee after the meeting."

"Why didn't you call?" He was coming on too strong but didn't know how to stop the raging emotions boiling in him.

"I tried. My phone battery died," she said over her shoulder as she passed him on her way through the door.

"Something could have happened to you. I didn't know where you were."

She turned to face him. "Yes, it could have but it didn't. I came and went without any problem before I knew you. I can take care of myself now as well."

"Yes, but that's before Marko started making threats."

"Look." She lifted her hands, letting her purse and the papers she carried fall to the floor. "I'm home safe."

He'd pushed too far and now she was pushing back. Worry and anxiety had done a number on him. Didn't she understand his distress at not knowing where she was?

"Kiefer, I don't think this is going to work. I can't take you hovering over me. Being on call to you. You reprimanding me when I don't show up on your timetable. I need the space and you can't seem to give it."

Had someone punched him in the stomach? He couldn't breathe. "Why? Because you can't understand that after what has happened, you need to be careful?" he spit. He hadn't talked to his ex-wife with such harshness even when he'd caught her kissing his best friend. Didn't Ashley understand that all this anger came from being concerned about her?

"No, because all you can think about is being that kid who didn't protect his mother. So now you overreact when you think someone might be in danger."

"Might? Like someone being shot at? That's a real danger. At least everyone but you thinks so."

She paused for a moment. "I know, I shouldn't ignore what happened. That's why I haven't made more of a fuss about the security men being here at night. But what I can't live with is this hyper-vigilance from you about where I am and when I'm coming home. I had enough of that during my childhood."

"But you've gone overboard the other way. Your parents convinced you that someone was out to get you at every turn. Now you believe no one will harm you. You take chances. Like facing up to Marko. Coming home at a late hour by yourself as if no one would be waiting to do you harm. You've been lucky so far. All I'm asking for is a simple phone call to let me know you aren't in a ditch somewhere."

"Not being a little overdramatic, are you? You think everyone is out to get me because the man your mother trusted turned on her. Your wife and friend betrayed you. You have to trust in people and believe in the best in them. My parents couldn't do it and I hated that."

"Trust. Is that what you were doing when you lied to your friends about being shot? Refused to tell your parents? If you would do that to the people you're closest to, how do I know I can trust you to act safely?"

"I would never purposely hurt you by putting myself in danger. I need you to trust me to make my own choices. I know you have a hard time with that and you have a good reason."

"But you're not being safe."

She took a step toward him. "How can you say that?"

"Because you're so caught up in doing and fixing for everyone else that you can't see what you should be doing for yourself. It's like you think that if you keep busy, pushing for an improvement here and rebuilding there, you won't have to think about what could happen or did happen. You want things to be perfect so another little girl won't be hurt. The world has depraved people in it, Ashley. You can't save everyone. Even Marko you're trying to save by not wanting to get police help. Some people are just bad."

She stepped toward him. "Like the guy that beat your mother. Your ex-wife. You want to carry the burden of hurt and guilt where they are concerned. You need to face that they were just bad people also. It seems like you might have the same problem as I do."

That statement hit home. "This isn't about what happened to my mother or with my ex-wife and what she did to me." He pointed to her and then to his chest. "This is about you and me. Why can't I get through to you? I'm not just worried about what happened tonight but your attitude about being aware of what is happening. It's as if you can't accept that someone has tried to do you harm. You seem to have gone into a mental shell where you're pretending you're unshakable. You're denying reality. Is that what you did after Lizzy went missing? Did you zone out so that you could deal with it? Look at you—you still wear your guilt around your neck."

Ashley fingered her necklace.

He couldn't stop himself. "You didn't hurt Lizzy. That guy did. You want me to move on but you haven't. You're still trying to make amends. Guess what, Ashley? You can't. You just have to live with what happened. You also can't save everyone."

She glared at him. "Like you do?"

That deflated him, his anger vented. "Maybe you're right." He hated to admit it. "Our issues are too large for us to get past."

Ashley's heart was splitting in two. It was excruciatingly painful. She didn't want to lose Kiefer but she didn't know what to do to hold on to him either. Giving up the freedom she'd fought so hard for wasn't easy.

Somehow she managed to say in a calm voice, "It's been a good ride while it lasted, Kiefer. I'm not going to change. You can't either. I wish you the best."

He stepped back, his shoulders slumped. "Then I should resign from the clinic."

Panic filled her. "Are you trying to blackmail me?" She needed him to work at the clinic. Only with a doctor would the clinic be successful. The council would want to know why if he did leave.

"No. I just don't think we can maintain a daily professional relationship after this. You're more to me than an associate and I'll never get past that. We obviously disagree fundamentally. It would be harmful for the clinic and what you're trying to do here."

"You talk about trust," she spit. "I trusted you to see the bigger picture. The one beyond us. You're no different than all the other people who come here for a few days then leave feeling good about themselves without truly investing in the neighborhood. Southriver is just something to look good on your résumé. I thought you were starting to devote your heart and life to this place. I believed, of all people, you understood loyalty. You were getting to know the people. Becoming part of us. Now here at the first bump you're trying to figure out how to get out."

"What're you talking about? *You* are more than a bump to me. I came here and worked my butt off, giving my all to the job. Not everyone wants or needs to spend every waking hour trying to save Southriver. You know what I think? I think you *need* to have a crusade. Something that will fill the void where you should have a personal life. You're afraid to care about anyone because you might lose them."

His accusation froze her for a moment. Was she really doing that? Was she covering up being scared? Pushing him away? But what was he offering her? The same thing they had been doing? There was no real commitment there.

She started picking the stuff up off the floor. "I just want people to have a happy life."

"It's not your job to provide that for them. Yours is to represent them. You're thinking only of Southriver and leaving no room for yourself. Me."

Had she really become consumed by her ideals? "I know it isn't working between us but I still need you to stay at the clinic. I was given six months to prove this clinic should be funded. If you leave now they'll pull my funding. Close the clinic. It'll affect my reelection as well."

That stuck like a knife in Kiefer's gut. Just as he'd suspected. It was about political gain. Once again he'd been fooled on more than one front. "That's all you care about. Your clinic. I thought we had something real and all you can say when

I tell you I'll be leaving is what's going to happen to your precious clinic. Tell me how you're so different from my ex-wife. All that talk of her being selfish. Even if the cause is a good one, it's still more important to you than us. I've played second seat for the last time to the last person I'm going to. I knew better than to get involved. But I let myself do it anyway. No more. Not again."

"I'm sorry you feel that way." Ashley put the papers and purse on the kitchen table. She sounded casual but all she wanted to do was drop to her knees and sob.

Kiefer walked toward her bedroom and returned with his shoes on and a bag in his hands. "I'll stay at the clinic until a replacement can be found."

"Thank you for that."

"Good-bye, Ashley."

"Bye." The word was weak and sad, just like how she felt.

The next few weeks were beyond painful for Ashley. Just knowing that Kiefer was only steps away made life almost unbearable. Still, she couldn't come up with a way to make the situation better. Surely a new doctor, an old and stodgy one, would replace Kiefer soon. She desperately wanted the clinic to succeed, but how she was going to survive when he was gone forever she had no idea.

She tried to force herself not to look out the window when it was time for Kiefer to leave for the day, but most of the time she couldn't resist just watching his back as he walked to his truck. The trick was to make sure she moved away from the window so he wouldn't see how pathetic she was if he happened to look up toward her apartment. The first week after their split she'd made a point of not returning home before she thought he would be done for the day. For the most part it had worked, but then she was driven to have just a glimpse of him whenever she could.

Did he ever do that? From what she could tell, he was honoring her request to avoid any contact outside of what was necessary for the clinic. Which had been little. He was an excellent administrator and the clinic was running smoothly. Ashley just hoped it wouldn't be damaged by Kiefer leaving. The community had started accepting him. It was ironic that her personal issue with Kiefer might ultimately damage what she had worked for years to accomplish in Southriver.

The time came when she had no choice but to go to the clinic. It had been open for weeks now and she needed to submit an updated report to the council about how it was doing. She hoped she could see Maria to get some statistics and be gone before she had to face Kiefer. Going in the front door instead of down her stairs seemed like the best way to accomplish that.

With purse in hand, she entered. The waiting room was full. She hated it that so many people felt ill, but it also demonstrated the need for the clinic. Kiefer was nowhere in sight as she approached the desk.

"Hey, Maria. I need to get an idea of how many patients have been seen since the clinic opened. How many were serious enough to send to the hospital and what the needs are."

"Wouldn't you rather talk to Dr. Bradford about that?"

Ashley glanced down the hall. Could she be a bigger coward? "No, I don't want to bother him. You should have all the information I need in your computer files."

"Sure, I'll pull it up if all you want is numbers. Problems and needs you'll have to talk to him about."

Ashley waited impatiently, all too aware that Kiefer could walk in at any moment. She believed in facing life head-on, yet she was hiding from the very person she cared the most about. A fact that had become agonizingly obvious to her over the last few days. What to do about it she didn't have an answer to.

The clinic door opened behind her.

"Oh, no," Maria whispered.

Ashley turned. Marko stood there with a wild look in his eyes and a gun in his hand. He slammed the door and locked it behind him.

Ashley's heart beat faster and fear lodged in her throat.

"No one move. Keep your hands where I can see them," Marko snarled. "Everyone that has a cell phone, take them out and put them on the floor. You two get over here." He pointed to her and Maria, gesturing that they join the others in the waiting area. "Cell phones on the floor."

They did as they were told. It sounded and

looked like a bad movie drama. But this was sickeningly real.

Marko pointed the gun at Ashley and commanded Maria, "Get the doctor."

"Marko, I'm sure Dr. Bradford will be glad to see you." Ashley worked to keep her voice level. "Put the gun down and I'll get him for you."

An older man sitting in the waiting room stood. Marko rounded on him.

"Sit down. Now." The man hesitated a second. Marko raised the gun. "Sit down now." He turned back to Ashley. "Call the doctor." The last word was a shout.

Before Ashley had a chance to move, Kiefer came hurrying up the hall. "What's going on here?"

He stopped short when he saw Marko.

"You're coming with me," Marko stated. He pointed the gun toward Kiefer's chest. "Let's go."

Ashley's heart missed a beat and she held her breath. What if Marko shot Kiefer? It was her fault Kiefer was in danger. She should have told the police weeks ago about Marko's threats.

"Where?" Kiefer asked. There was a note of defiance in his voice.

"You don't need to know." Marko waved the gun toward the door.

"I'm not going anywhere until I know what this is about." Kiefer's voice was firm.

Marko pointed the gun at Ashley. "Let's go or I'll shoot her."

Kiefer's jaw tightened, his lips thinned. Pain filled his eyes. "I need to get my bag. If you'll tell me what this is about, I can get the correct supplies."

Marko took a second before he answered. "Knife wound. You stay here. She can get the supplies." He pointed the gun at Maria.

She was in tears. Quaking, she looked as if she might become hysterical at any moment. Her voice wobbled when she said, "I can't. I don't know what to get."

Marko looked at her for a moment then turned to Ashley. "You do it. Don't try anything. All of you, let's go." He directed the gun toward the waiting room.

The group stood and headed down the hall. Ashley followed with Kiefer close behind.

"Get in that room. All of you."

As Ashley started to crowd into the full exam

room with everyone else, Marko said, "Not you. You're going with us."

"She doesn't need to go. You have me," Kiefer said.

"Shut up. She'll be my insurance. You do what you're told and don't try anything."

"You already have me. Leave her." Kiefer sounded as if he were about to beg.

"I said shut up. You don't make the rules here." To the people in the exam room he said, "First person who opens this door will be shot." He pulled the door to the exam room closed. He looked at Ashley. "You get what's needed."

"I don't know what that is. I'm not a nurse."

Marko looked at Kiefer. "You tell her what to get from here."

Ashley went into the supply room while Kiefer remained in the hall.

"My bag is on the floor by the desk. Open it and I'll tell you what to put in."

Ashley found his backpack behind the desk and faced Kiefer, who stood at the door. With her hands shaking, she bent to pick it up. Opening the pack, she placed it on the desk chair.

This wasn't the Marko she'd known. Why hadn't

she listened to Kiefer? Had she been so caught up in what she'd wanted that she'd been unable to see anything else? She would die if anything happened to Kiefer. She couldn't live if she was the cause of him getting hurt.

*His phone.*

It was under a stack of papers on his desk. She glanced at Kiefer. His gaze met hers. He shifted, drawing Marko's attention.

Marko shouted, "Be still!"

With her heart in her throat and all the possibilities of what might go wrong swirling in her head, she acted as if she was surprised and knocked the papers off, making sure the phone fell into the pack. Now all she had to do was pray that the phone didn't ring.

"Hurry up," Marko growled.

Ashley gathered the supplies as Kiefer listed them, shoving them into the bag.

"Let's go," Marko announced.

Ashley zipped up the bag and joined Kiefer in the hall. He took it from her. Pulling it over one shoulder, he turned to go toward the front door.

"No, the other way. Up the back stairs."

Marko pushed Kiefer forward. "Doctor, you first."

"Marko," Ashley said, "you know this is kidnapping. A federal offense. If you stop now, Dr. Bradford and I won't press any charges."

"She's right, Marko."

This time Marko gave her a shove. "Both of you shut up and get moving."

Kiefer didn't look pleased but he didn't argue further. Ashley climbed the stairs behind Kiefer, all too aware of Marko's gun aimed at her back. She glanced at the bat still standing at the top of the stairs, hoping Kiefer wouldn't be a hero and pick it up. Thankfully he didn't.

In her kitchen Marko said, "Let's go. Down the back steps."

Again Kiefer led the way. At the bottom of the steps Marko said, "Now through that hole in the fence. Doctor, you first."

Ashley stepped through after Kiefer. Her pants leg caught on the broken wire. Kiefer snatched her up before she fell, bringing her hard against him. Just the feel of him eased her fear.

"Get moving," Marko snarled.

Kiefer released her. She moved ahead of him

and Marko made no complaint. They followed a path through the vacant lot behind her building. The knee-high grass pulled against her legs. Her pumps sank into the sandy ground. A couple of times Kiefer supported her with a hand to her arm, helping her to stay on her feet.

Halfway across the lot Kiefer asked Marko, "Why don't you release Ashley? I'll go with you with no complaints."

Ashley wanted to scream no. He could be killed. Maybe she could talk some sense into Marko. He would never listen to Kiefer.

"Shut up and keep moving," Marko growled.

At the next block Marko directed them to a waiting car. "Ashley, get in the front seat. Doctor, in the back. I'll shoot her if you give me any trouble," he said pointedly to Kiefer.

When the doors were shut behind them, the driver passed a dark T-shirt to her and one over the seat to Kiefer. Marko said, "Put it on your head. Make sure to cover your face."

Ashley did as she was told. The stench of body odor almost made her gag but she pulled the shirt in place. She hardly had it situated before the car lurched forward.

For what seemed like forever they wove in and out of streets, taking corners too fast. She held on to the door handle, trying to stay upright. Where were they going? They had traveled so far that they could no longer be in Southriver.

A tugboat horn blew. They were near the river. They bumped over railroad tracks a couple of times so hard that Ashley's head almost hit the roof. They made a final turn and the car came to a screeching halt, slamming Ashley forward.

"Ashley, are you okay?" Kiefer's voice was muffled under his shirt.

"I'm fine."

"Shut up. Pull those shirts off your heads and get out," Marko ordered.

Doing so, she saw they were inside a warehouse. There were boxes stacked to the roof and empty wooden pallets on the floor. After the harrowing ride, she climbed out of the car on shaky legs. Kiefer joined her with his bag in hand.

"This way." Marko indicated some type of office-looking area in one corner of the huge building. Lit from within, it had one door, and windows made up half the walls.

The driver jerked her toward Kiefer when she

didn't move. They walked side by side with Marko behind them.

"Tell me what's going on," Kiefer demanded.

"You'll see soon enough," Marko said.

The driver opened the door to the office and Ashley, then Kiefer with Marko behind him, entered. Inside was a man lying on a dirty mattress that had no cover on it on an old metal bed frame. Based on the amount of bloody rags on the floor, he'd lost a large amount of blood. His pallor was deathly white.

Kiefer hurried to the bedside in full doctor mode. Slipping the bag from his shoulder and setting it on the floor, he unzipped it, found plastic gloves and pulled them on. He lifted the material that looked like a T-shirt from the wound in the man's midsection.

The man moaned.

"I'm Dr. Bradford. I'm here to help you. I'm going to have a look at you and then I'll give you something for pain. What's your name?"

"Jorge," he said in little more than a whisper.

"He needs to be in a hospital," Kiefer said to Marko.

"No," Marko barked.

Ashley watched Kiefer look into Jorge's eyes. His hand went to the young man's forehead. "He needs surgery. He's running a fever. Has lost too much blood."

"You take care of him here," Marko said.

"He's already on the road to an infection." Kiefer looked around the filthy area. "Sewing him up here will only make it worse."

Marko pointed the gun at her. "You'll do it."

Kiefer glanced away but his look returned to meet hers. There was pain, worry and resignation in his eyes. "I'll need your help, Ashley."

"I've never done anything like this." She couldn't keep the quiver of fear out of her voice.

He gave her a reassuring smile. "I'll tell you what to do every step of the way. I have complete faith you can handle it." Kiefer looked around. "Is there water?"

"In there." Marko nodded toward a door.

Kiefer looked back at her. "See if you can find something to put some water in. If not…" he pulled a bag of bandage pads out of the backpack and handed them to her "…wet these." He gave her another reassuring smile that didn't reach his eyes.

"I'm sorry," she mouthed to him.

He nodded and turned back to his patient.

Marko leaned against the wall where he could see both of them. "Get busy." To his driver he said, "You go watch outside."

The guy left.

Ashley went to a door that she guessed led to a bathroom. It turned out to be a small kitchen area and there was a bath off that. The place was nasty. Apparently someone had been living there for a few days, if not longer. Open food packages were everywhere. How was she supposed to find anything in here sanitary enough to hold water? Searching under the sink, she located a mop bucket, and pulling it out, she put it under the sink faucet. The water ran brown.

"Yuck." She jerked the bucket out from under the tap, emptied it while leaving the water running, then waited for the water to turn clear.

Marko stuck his head in the door. "Get busy."

"I am. Everything in this place is nasty. Marko, let us take your friend to the hospital. He's going to die if you don't."

"No more talking. Get busy."

The water had started to run clearer and she shoved the bucket under the faucet again. Using her hand, Ashley washed the bucket the best she could. With it full, she carried it back to Kiefer and set it down next to him. He glanced at her as he continued to apply pressure to the patient's abdomen. "Good girl. I need you to go around to the other side of the bed."

It had been moved into the middle of the room.

"Take my bag. Pull that chair up close and put the supplies on it." He indicated the wooden straight-backed chair behind a metal desk.

This could be her chance. If she could just figure out some way to use the phone. Glancing at Marko, she then looked at Kiefer. His expression said clearly that he trusted her. That he knew she would do what was necessary. She wouldn't disappoint him. Wouldn't let him down this time. Ashley went to her knees beside the bed and started pulling supplies out.

"I'm going to need the scissors first and the bandages."

She removed items until she found what Kiefer had requested. Her fingers brushed the cell phone as she pulled a box from the pack. Could she push numbers without Marko noticing? No, the time wasn't right. She'd have one chance and she would need to make that count. She handed Kiefer the scissors and bandages.

"I'm going to need a suture kit and the bottle of saline."

As he cut away the man's shirt and started to clean around the wound, Ashley continued to unload the backpack. Thankfully she had Kiefer and the bed between her and Marko. If she could just slip the phone out far enough to touch 911… Her heart beat faster as she reached into the backpack again. Her fingers circled the phone. Her hand shook. She gave a quick glance at Marko. He was still glaring at them, watching too closely. Not yet. She laid the backpack flat on the floor, setting the phone close to the zipper opening.

"I'm ready to suture. I'm going to need your help. Put some gloves on," Kiefer said.

Ashley did so. Her fear must have shown on her face because he reached across and squeezed her hand. "We'll get through this."

"Stop all the talking and get going," Marko said, shifting impatiently.

Kiefer put a hand on their patient's shoulder. "Jorge, I don't have any way of making you more comfortable. I'm sorry. This is going to hurt." He said to Ashley in a resigned tone, "Please open one of the suture packages."

Over the next hour she watched as Kiefer meticulously closed the wound. Jorge groaned through the first few stitches then passed out. Kiefer said little other than to occasionally tell her to move a finger here or dab a bandage there as he worked. If she hadn't known he was a good doctor already, she had no doubt of his abilities now.

Kiefer looked back at Marko. "That's the best I can do under the circumstances. He needs antibiotics that I don't have. If he doesn't get them soon I can't promise what will happen. We'll just have to wait and see. If you really care about Jorge you would take him to the hospital."

Marko snorted, "And go to jail. That's not going to happen."

Ashley started cleaning up the area. There were a few supplies left to pack away. Pulling the backpack to her, she was careful not to knock the phone out of the bag. Bumping the chair, she caused what was left of the supplies to fall off. Leaning over, she acted as if she was gathering the supplies. She pulled the opening of the pack back and touched 911.

"What's the deal over there?" Marko commanded.

She reached under the bed. "Nothing. I'm just getting a box."

Ashley's breath caught in horror. She hadn't changed the volume. Opening the bag, hoping Marko thought she was storing the box, she found the phone again. Fumbling, she searched for the buttons on the side of the phone and pushed the bottom one.

"What're you doing? Give me that." Marko headed in her direction.

Ashley palmed the phone.

Kiefer took that moment to stand, bumping against Marko. It gave her time to push the phone under the mattress.

"Get out of the way. I should kill you." Marko pushed Kiefer.

Pain swamped her. She wouldn't survive if something happened to Kiefer.

"Give me that." Marko pointed the gun toward the backpack. "What do you have in there?"

"Nothing but the supplies the doctor told me to put in here," she said as evenly as she could.

Marko jerked it out of her hand and dumped

the contents on the floor, kicking them around. "I said not to try anything."

"Look for yourself. There's nothing there." Kiefer came around the end of the bed and offered her a hand.

She slowly rose, her knees stiff from being on the concrete floor for so long.

"What're you doing?" Marko growled.

"Helping Ashley up. We both need to stand. We've been kneeling a long time." Kiefer gave Marko a defiant look. "So what's the plan now? The police will be looking for us. Jorge shouldn't be moved. You're stuck. You need to turn yourself in. Why don't you let Ashley go and get help?"

Kiefer was still trying to protect her. She appreciated it but she wouldn't leave him. This was all happening because of her. Why couldn't she have accepted Kiefer's warnings that Marko was a threat? She'd give anything to turn back time, make this go away. Have her and Kiefer returned to the intimacy they'd shared. If they got out of this she would do everything in her power to make it up to him.

"No more talking. Get over there and be quiet. I need to think." Marko pointed to a corner.

Kiefer held her hand as they moved to the farthest spot from the door. They stood against the wall. Her knees were just starting to recover.

The driver of the car came in and Marko conferred with him too low for her to hear, glancing at them a couple of times.

Kiefer turned slightly, putting his back to them. His mouth came close to her ear. "Phone?"

Ashley nodded briefly as she watched Jorge. Kiefer's brows went up in question. She mouthed, "Under the mattress."

## CHAPTER NINE

KIEFER SLID DOWN the wall to sit on the floor. He tugged on Ashley's hand, encouraging her to join him. She did, coming shoulder to shoulder with him. They were both tired physically and emotionally. Fear had fed an adrenaline rush. Now that it dropped, exhaustion took over. Neither extremes were healthy.

They needed to get to the phone somehow. Finding the right time was going to be the tough part. If Marko would only leave the room. Getting Ashley to safety was his top priority. There was no way of knowing if her 911 message had gone through. He wrapped his arm around her shoulders and pulled her close.

Ashley looked up at him with those big eyes full of misery. "I'm so sorry I got you into this." Emotion was thick in her voice. "I should've listened to you when Marko came into my house. I thought I saw him that night I was shot but I didn't say anything."

She was such an idealistic soul. That was part of the reason he loved her and yet shouldn't. It didn't matter now. He gave her shoulder a squeeze and kissed her temple. "We'll get out of this. We'll be fine. Hang in there."

"I hope so. I owe you big-time."

He gave her a wry smile. "And I plan to collect."

"Shut up, you two! I need to think." Marco pulled the chair out from around the bed and put it in front of the closed door.

"It looks like we're going to be here awhile," Kiefer whispered. "We might as well get some sleep." He stretched out his legs.

"Thank you for all you have done. You were amazing."

"Shush. Sleep."

Ashley laid her head against his shoulder. It wasn't long until she was breathing evenly. He was glad to have her in his arms again but this wasn't the way he'd wanted it to happen.

Somebody kicked his foot, jiggling him awake. Kiefer didn't know how much time had gone by but he guessed it was in the early morning hours.

He looked over at Ashley. Her eyes were open. Fear filled them.

"Tell me what kinds of antibiotics Jorge needs," Marko demanded from above them.

"Jorge needs to be in the hospital, getting intravenous ones," Kiefer said.

"That's not going to happen. What're the names?"

Kiefer named off a few common antibiotics. "They won't be strong enough to keep the infection under control. He needs to be in a hospital."

Marko's face became distorted and he pointed the gun at him. "Shut up about the hospital. He's not going. Do. Not. Say. It. Again. Stand up. Both of you."

Kiefer stood and then helped Ashley to her feet. Marco reached behind his back and pulled out plastic wire fasteners. "Turn around."

They did as he instructed. Marko fastened Kiefer's wrists together behind his back and did the same to Ashley's. He then used another band to attach them together at the hands, so that they were back to back.

"I'll be back." With that he kicked the chair out of the way and left. The door clicked shut behind him.

Kiefer whispered. "Let's wait until we're sure he's gone."

They stood not moving. Waiting. Listening.

"Let's check the door first then go after the phone," Kiefer said. "I'll walk forward if you can go backward."

There were a few missteps and a wobble back and forth until they found a rhythm. They made it to the door.

"Turn sideways and slide up next to the door and let's see if we can get our hands on it."

Ashley did just as he asked. Kiefer managed to reach the knob. It didn't open. "Okay, let's go after the phone. You forward this time and I'll follow."

Skirting the bed, Ashley led them to the spot where she'd left the phone.

"I don't know how we're going to do this," she said.

"Back up as close to me as you can. We're going to push against each other as we squat down. I want you to reach out and get the phone." This plan had to work. He needed to get Ashley out of there.

"What about Jorge?"

"He's passed out. Even if he wakes he's too

weak to move. The best way to help him is for us to get out of here." Urgency filled him.

Kiefer waited until she'd pressed her back against his.

"On three let's go down. One, two, three." Slowly they moved toward the floor. Ashley pulled on his arms. His right shoulder strained to a painful point before she said, "I have my fingers on it."

Thump. The phone hitting the floor told him she had at least removed it from under the mattress.

"Okay, let's go up. Push hard against me and take small steps backward." They worked themselves to a standing position.

"Now we have to get it off the floor." Ashley moaned. "Marko could already be on his way back."

"Let's not worry about that. Let's go down again and this time I'll reach for the phone. The more you lean on me the easier it'll be for you." He waited until she pushed against him. "Go." They worked their way toward the floor. Kiefer's thighs burned as he went into a squat. Ashley groaned behind him. "Just a little more. I almost have it."

Relief filled him when his fingers circled the

phone. "Let's go up. Not too fast or we'll fall." It was a slow process but they made it to a standing position again. "Swing your arms to the left." Ashley did as he asked. Looking over his shoulder, he touched the screen of the phone. It still remained black. Disappointment washed over him.

"The battery is dead." The words were a cry of anguish from Ashley as she looked back.

"Well, we can't depend on that. We've got to get out of these handcuffs then out of this room." He swung the phone so that it landed on the bed at Jorge's feet. "Let's go see what we can find in the kitchen. Lady's choice—do you want to walk backward or forward?"

"I'll take forwards. You ready?"

"Lead on." At least he'd got a small chuckle out of her.

They shuffled their way into the kitchen.

"Okay, let's start with the easy stuff and look through the drawers first," Kiefer said. They slid sideways to the counter. "Let's get it open."

It took some maneuvering but they soon had a drawer open. Nothing. They shuffled to the next one and then the next. It wasn't until his face and body were pressed against the wall and they had the last drawer open that there was a sliver of hope.

"I'm touching something." The excitement in Ashley's voice made his optimism soar. "I think it's an old dinner knife."

Kiefer held his position. "Get it out but don't drop it, whatever you do."

"I've got it. I've got it."

He felt the metal across the top of one hand. "Let me hold it."

"You don't trust me?"

There was the old Ashley he knew so well. He trusted her more than anyone else he knew. "Yes, but I want you to cut your strap off. How sharp is it?"

"Not very, but it does have some serrations."

"That's better than nothing. Get started." He held the knife while she worked her hands into position.

Moving her wrist back and forth, she pushed against the knife. "This is taking too long."

"Just keep at it. We don't have a choice."

After an agonizing amount of time, the plastic finally broke. Ashley's hands were free.

"Now I'll do you." She had already taken the knife from him.

"No, it takes too long. We need to look for a way out of here. Go see if you can open the door."

She hurried out of the room and he followed. Ashley pulled on the doorknob. It wasn't budging.

"Check the bathroom. See if it has a window to the outside."

Again Ashley rushed from the room. Kiefer stood looking at the structure of the door. The hinges didn't have pins. They were stuck.

"Kiefer, come here. There's a window."

He hurried to her.

"It's not a very big one but I think I could get through it." She was already standing on the commode, pushing at the window.

"You need to break it out. Pull off your jacket and wrap it around your hand. Pull your shirt over your face so that you don't get hit by any glass."

She did as he said and started striking the glass. It broke with a large crash.

"Now make sure all the edges are gone."

Ashley worked her material-covered hand around the window frame. She stuck her head out the window. "It's to the outside." Excitement filled her voice. "Now let's get your hands undone."

"No, you're going through the window. I couldn't get through it anyway. I need to stay with Jorge."

"No, Kiefer. No!"

His look met hers. "You're going after help. Now stop complaining and get moving. Climb up my back and wrap your arms around my neck. Then I want you to put your feet through the window, otherwise you would be going headfirst and I don't want you to hurt that pretty head."

She reached up and cupped his face, pulling his mouth to hers. Kiefer's heart jumped. He'd missed her kisses. Thirsted for them. He pulled back. "Quit taking advantage of a man with his hands tied behind his back and get going."

Ashley gave him a weak smile then stood on the commode to get into position. Kiefer backed up and straddled the commode. Ashley put her arms around his neck from behind and pulled herself up his back. Kiefer leaned forward as her body weight pushed against him. She lifted her feet, putting them through the opening.

She was halfway out the window when he turned around. "Run for the nearest lit area. I'll be

ight here waiting when you get back. Now, get."
His gaze held hers until she dropped out of sight.

He wanted to say so much more but they were
running out of time.

Ashley sprinted until her breaths were deep and
her side hurt. Her blouse stuck to her in the warm,
muggy night. Her feet throbbed from running in
her pumps. She was in the warehouse district of
the shipping area of Savannah. There was no life
around, only the occasional dim security light. If
Marko returned to find her gone he'd come looking for her. Surely kill Kiefer. A sick feeling filled
her. That wasn't going to happen.

She ran again. Surely she would find someone
soon. Wouldn't let herself think any differently.
Headlights came toward her.

Joy made her heart jump. *Help!*

She stumbled and fell, pushed her way up again.
Waving her hands back and forth above her head,
she signaled for them to stop. A sick feeling hit
her. For a second she dropped her arms. What if
it was Marko? But what if it was help and they
passed her by because they didn't see her? She
had to take a chance.

Waving again, she watched as the car accelerated then pulled to a screeching halt beside her. With relief that almost had her on her knees again, Ashley saw it was a police car. A uniformed officer hopped out of the car. It was Bull. She fell into his arms.

"Help! Kiefer is locked in a warehouse. Marko kidnapped us. Call an ambulance. There's an injured man in there too."

"Get in. Show us where." He opened the back passenger door and Ashley climbed in. The policeman driving was already on the radio, letting other patrolmen know they needed help. When Bull was back in the car the driver stepped on the gas.

She sat forward, looking through the wire mesh and out the windshield. Could she recall enough to find the correct building? They all looked the same in the dark. She had to remember. Had to get the right one. Kiefer's life depended on it.

"It's down here. The third big building on the right. No, fourth. I came out between those buildings." She pointed off to the right despite the fact no one could see her do it. "The one with the trash cans beside it."

The patrolman stopped the car in front of the large roll-down door.

"You stay here," Bull said, as he leaped out and pulled his gun. The sound of sirens filled the air.

She watched as Bull and the other officer opened a smaller door beside the larger one and entered the warehouse. Watching with her nose pressed against the window, she waited. Time seemed to slow to a crawl. More police cars arrived and men flooded in. Still no Kiefer. Where was he? Was he all right? Panic became a living thing in her. She hung on to the edge of the car door and didn't take her eyes off the opening to the warehouse. Was this how Kiefer had felt when he'd been waiting for her that night? Tears filled her eyes.

Had Marko returned while she'd been gone? She couldn't think like that. Not now that she'd found help.

An ambulance pulled to a stop nearby. The EMTs unloaded a gurney and pushed it through the larger door, which was opening. Soon after Bull came out of the building and walked toward her. He opened the door.

"Kiefer?" She was almost afraid of the answer.

"Inside. He's fine. Asking to see you."

Ashley ran into the building and stopped. Kiefer walked toward her.

Happiness surged through her. She smiled as the band squeezing her heart popped open. She ran, tears streaming down her face, toward him. His arms opened wide. When she reached him he engulfed her, lifting her off her feet. Kiefer was solid, sure and safe. Best of all—alive. She never wanted to leave him again.

"I thought… Thought…I was so scared…"

He held her tight as if he never wanted to let her go. "Shh, sweetheart. I'm fine. You did good. I couldn't have asked for a better partner." Kiefer slowly placed her on her feet and looked at her. He studied her as if making sure she really was okay.

"Did Marko come back?"

"No, but Bull can tell you all about that. I have to go to the hospital with Jorge. I want you to go too and be checked out. Bull is going to see that you get to your parents'. No argument."

She would go gladly. If Kiefer wasn't going to be with her then she wanted people around her who made her feel safe. Her parents could provide that. Despite them hovering when she'd been a child, she had felt secure. Smiling up at him, she nodded. "No argument."

The emergency crew came past them with Jorge on a gurney.

"I've got to go." He gave her a quick kiss and followed Jorge into the back of the ambulance.

Bull joined her. "Come on. I'll get you to the hospital and call your parents."

Ashley slowly walked to the car with Bull. Kiefer had said nothing about seeing her again. Had anything really changed between them?

It had been three days and still Kiefer hadn't called. Ashley had begun to worry that he wouldn't.

Her parents had picked her up from the hospital. Her arm had been put in a sling again. Not because of her gunshot injury but because her shoulder had been hurt from being hyperextended when she and Kiefer had been tied together.

Bull had explained on the way to the hospital that 911 had received the call, but before they could pinpoint the location, the battery had gone dead. All they'd had was a vicinity. When they had been called to a break-in at a pharmacy, they'd suspected it was related but they'd still had a large area to cover. They'd started searching the area. That was when they'd found her. On the way to the hospital the call came through that Marko and his driver had been picked up.

By the time her mother and father had made it to the hospital they had been typical worried parents. This time Ashley had found it comforting. She'd appreciated the pampering, even though Kiefer hadn't been there to offer some as well.

The second day she was at her parents' she went for a walk along her old block. It was warm outside but not hot and steamy yet. It was summertime and children were playing in their yards.

She stopped and looked at the house next door. The one Ron had lived in years before. After what he'd done, his parents had moved away, no longer able to face their shame. The new neighbors had painted the place, but it still held the stigma of being where Ron had lived. How could anyone have known? Was there ever a way of knowing what people were capable of? Not really. Mostly she had to just believe in the goodness of mankind. That trust was something she'd had a hard time giving. Kiefer had more than earned it. Proved himself worthy.

Still, she had misjudged Marko. No, that wasn't true. She just hadn't wanted to see it. He had given her all the signs.

Ashley continued along the street, lifting her face so that the sun warmed it. It had been a while since she had really looked at the area. Little had changed yet somehow it seemed different. She went on another couple of blocks and turned right. There was her father's small grocery store. Entering, she saw her father behind the counter.

"Hey, sweetheart. It's nice to see you."

"Hi."

"How about a drink?" He walked toward an old soda machine.

"That would be great." She accepted the bottle from him.

"I'm not busy this morning, so come have a seat and stay a minute." He indicated a stool nearby.

Ashley took it and her father the other.

"How're you feeling?"

"Better. Much better. In fact, I think I'll be going home tomorrow." She took a sip of her soda.

"It's been nice having you but I know you have your own life."

Ashley nodded.

"I'm sorry about what happened to you. I never would've thought Marko would do such a thing." A dark look came over his face. "But then, I've made that mistake before. I know you had a hard time with how overprotective I was when you were a kid. It was only because I loved you."

Had her father felt the same way she had when Marko had pointed the gun at Kiefer? Or when she'd had to leave him behind, knowing Marko could return at any moment? Had that been the same alarm that had consumed Kiefer when she'd been shot?

She'd experienced that type of fear. "I understand that now, Dad."

"I hope so."

There had been no compromise with her father but Kiefer had offered one. Instead of accepting it, she'd all but slapped him in the face. She'd thrown away what could have been.

A customer entered. Her father kissed her on the forehead. "I love you, honey. It can make us act in strange ways."

"Yes, it can."

A few minutes later Ashley put the drink bottle down and left. She didn't return the way she had come but instead walked toward where Lizzy had lived. The house was still there but her family had moved away as well. Ashley stood looking at the house. In her mind she could see Lizzy running down the steps to meet her. Or jumping as she played hopscotch on the sidewalk where Ashley stood.

It was time to let go. Lizzy and what had happened to her had shaped her own past, but now it was time to find a future of her own making. Ignoring the pain in her arm, she reached up behind her neck and unlatched the necklace. It slipped into the other hand and she dropped it into her pocket. Kiefer was right. She needed to think about what she wanted and needed. And that was him. He was her future. If she could convince him to give her another chance.

Kiefer had wanted to go straight to Ashley's parents' house the second he left the hospital. He had called but she had been asleep. Her mother had assured him she was doing fine. Knowing she needed rest after their ordeal, he had decided to wait. He had things he had to get straight in his mind, in his life, before he went to Ashley and begged her to consider giving him another chance.

What he had learned was that life was unpredictable and could be cut short. Finding someone special was rare and worth fighting for. He hadn't been able to handle everything by himself during their situation with Marko, but with Ashley beside him they had made a great team. It was impossible to stop bad things from happening to her but he could be there to support her when they did. He'd not been able to protect his mother because he'd been a child. She didn't blame him and he shouldn't blame himself.

Ashley had told him more than once that he needed to face what had happened to his mother. He couldn't confront that man but he could face the man that had threatened Ashley.

The next day Kiefer sat on a metal jail chair in a cubicle, looking at Marko. After some fast talking on Kiefer's part, he had convinced Bull to arrange the meeting.

Kiefer picked up the phone on the wall. After a moment of hesitation Marko did the same.

Marko jerked his chin at Kiefer. "What do you want?"

"To tell you that your buddy Jorge is going to live. He'll spend some time in the hospital but he'll make it."

Marko shrugged from where he slumped in the chair. "Okay. So you could have sent a message. Why did you show up here?"

"Because I needed to face you. For you to see me on this side of the glass and know you are on that side. To tell you that you'll never again hold any power over me or Ashley. I'll be there to testify against you and when I'm done you'll be forgotten by me forever."

Marko bared his teeth. "You think I care."

"It doesn't matter to me. What does matter to me is Ashley. If you so much as say her name, I'll use everything in my power to see that you never see the light of day again." Kiefer pushed his chair back and stood. "Now, you have a good day."

Kiefer walked out into the sunlight. The day had just become brighter.

He rolled his shoulders and headed toward his car. As for Brittney and Josh, it was time to move beyond what they had done as well. They had been controlling his happiness and he wasn't going to give them that power anymore. They'd been allowed too much importance in his life for too long. He was tired of having others feel sorry for him and he was disgusted by how long he'd felt sorry for himself. He'd found something good in his life, and he was going to hang on for dear life.

Ashley would never betray him. She was loyal to a fault. To her community, her family and her friends. She would be the same to him as well. There wasn't a selfish bone in her body. She believed in commitment. Had proved that by her devotion to the people in her life. Ashley was the type of person he wanted beside him forever.

She had not only given him his self-esteem back but she'd given him a home. Not the sterile life that looked like his apartment but something comfortable like her place. He'd become part of Southriver in the short amount of time he'd worked at the clinic. People were no longer people who came and went. They were business owners, grandmothers, young families—friends. He'd had no idea he'd needed that until he'd had it and had been about to lose it. He needed South-river as much as it needed him.

Now it was time to convince Ashley that they be-longed together. That was going to require a gran-diose gesture. He had just such a thing in mind.

# CHAPTER TEN

ASHLEY GLANCED AT the crowd filling the city council meeting room. There were more people than usual attending. She spoke to another alderman, hoping to garner some support for the clinic. She was afraid she was going to have a fight on her hands.

Her and Kiefer's ordeal had made the news. She'd done numerous interviews. To her surprise she'd even seen one with Kiefer. She had fully anticipated him to dodge such a thing, but he'd given a good solid sound bite, glossing over what had happened to them and turning the focus on the efforts being made in the Southriver area and what he did at the clinic. He'd made an impressive spokesman.

Others on the council had also been interviewed. They had made it clear in one way or another that they weren't in support of the clinic or the methods being used to make improvements in Southriver.

Outside of seeing Kiefer on TV, she'd not seen him in ages. It hurt terribly. The clinic had been closed when she'd returned to her place. She had been told that Kiefer had been given some time off. He deserved that. She had also been informed that at this time there was no one to replace him. Ashley couldn't bring herself to ask any more questions. Whatever she had hoped for with the clinic and Kiefer was gone.

He'd not even called. Okay, that wasn't true. He had spoken to her mother, but that wasn't the same as him talking to her. All she could try to do now was accept what he wanted and that wasn't her.

All the media publicity had shone a light on Southriver, but it had been a negative one for the most part. That was a portion of what the council meeting was about tonight. The mayor and a couple of the aldermen wanted to rescind the funding. Their argument was that the city couldn't afford to take a chance that what had happened to Kiefer wouldn't happen to another doctor. The liability was too great.

As painful as it was for the clinic to close, losing Kiefer hurt far worse. It was a constant ache that didn't ease. More than once she'd been in her kitchen and had stopped what she'd been doing to look at the door to the stairs, thinking she'd heard his footsteps. It would take a long time for her to push memories of him out of her home and even longer for them to dim in her heart.

She couldn't think about that now. She had a council meeting to survive. A clinic and a neighborhood to protect.

"Okay, folks. Everybody find a seat. It's time for the meeting to begin," the city council chairman said, hitting the gavel on a block of wood.

A tingle went down her spine. She turned and looked out over the room. Kiefer had just entered. His gaze met hers and held. For Ashley all the activity in the room faded away. Her heart went into a wild pit-a-pat rhythm and her entire body hummed with awareness. Everything in her zeroed in on Kiefer.

"Alderman Marsh, if you'll take your seat we'll get started."

Ashley blinked. Warmth filled her face. Kiefer grinned. Her hand trembled as she pulled her chair out from under the table. When she looked up again Kiefer was no longer visible. Had he left? Searching, she found him sitting in a seat a couple of rows from the back.

What was he doing here?

The meeting was being called to order. Her focus was divided between what was being said and Kiefer. Normally she was a highly attentive woman where her work as alderman was concerned, but this evening all her focus was on the man who hadn't taken his eyes off her.

"Ms. Marsh, in light of what happened recently, we feel it's too risky to ask a doctor to work at the clinic," Alderman Richards, one of the council members, said.

That statement jerked her out of her Kiefer-induced trance. Alderman Henderson had been the most vocal about not supporting the clinic in the beginning. Now he was bringing others over to his side. She wasn't surprised he would be the one who would take advantage of the Marko incident to make his point.

"We can't let one problem close down the clinic. The people of Southriver should have the care they deserve," Ashley responded.

"Yes, but we can't expect the hospital to put

their doctors in harm's way by working there," another alderman said.

She looked across the table at the woman. "You do know I live in Southriver? Was raised there."

"Where you live is your choice. The city council asking the hospital to send a doctor there is ours. We don't want to put ourselves out there for a civil suit if he or she is hurt doing so," Alderman Richards said, pushing his wire-rimmed glasses back up his nose.

Ashley had heard all the political rhetoric before. "The people of Southriver deserve to keep the clinic. They were supporting it, using it and, more importantly, benefiting from it. More than once Dr. Bradford..." she looked at Kiefer "...identified medical problems that would have been left undiagnosed if the person hadn't come to the clinic. The patients would have never gone to the hospital until it was too late. He's even taken care of my mother when she had a severe burn. The clinic is making a difference. Will make a difference if we continue to support it. Close it and it will be the first step toward telling the people of Southriver they aren't worth the trouble.

They're part of this city just as the rest of the districts are and deserve to be treated that way."

"Thank you for that impassioned statement, but the problem still remains that the clinic was a scene of a kidnapping and the doctor was taken at gunpoint. We can't have that happen again or anything else criminal. The hospital isn't going to put their employees into that type of danger."

Kiefer stood. His gaze met hers before he looked at Alderman Richards. "I'm that doctor who was kidnapped. Dr. Kiefer Bradford. And I disagree with you. The hospital is going to continue to support the clinic. I am going to continue as director and hope to encourage an additional doctor to join me. I believe in Southriver and what Ms. Marsh is trying to do for the community. I ask that the council continue their support. But even if you don't, I'll still be practicing in Southriver. And the city council won't be able to take credit for the work being done there."

Ashley stared at Kiefer in amazement. She felt as though she had been picked up, whirled around and set down again. Kiefer was going to stay on at the clinic.

As elated as she was over him staying, she

didn't know how she was going to survive seeing him every day and knowing there could never be more than friendship between them. Somehow she would have to come to terms with that.

The city council chairman said, "I don't see how we can disagree with that offer. If Dr. Bradford wants to continue to run the clinic after what happened to him, then I don't see how we can refuse to support it. The clinic is working to make Savannah a better place. A better place to live and visit. What's good for Southriver would be good for Savannah."

How like Alderman Henderson to posture to the positive. He was up for reelection at the end of the year. More than once he'd swung to whatever side had best suited him. Thankfully this time it was hers.

"I call for a vote," Ashley said.

It passed unanimously and Ashley only half listened to what was discussed during the rest of the meeting. All she could think about was speaking to Kiefer. Trying to understand what he was doing. As soon as the meeting was over she headed directly to him.

She wanted to jump into his arms and kiss him

but she settled for smiling. "Thank you so much for what you're doing for the clinic."

"I'm not doing it just for the clinic. Can we go somewhere to talk?"

He could take her anywhere. "I'd like that. Let me get my purse. I'll be right back."

"I'm not going anywhere." He'd made the statement sound as if it had a deeper meaning.

As they walked out of the building Kiefer put his hand on the small of her back. A shiver went down her spine. She'd missed his touch. Any touch from him. They made their way to the parking deck.

"Did you mean what you said in there?" Ashley asked.

"Every word of it." There was no sound of wavering in his voice.

"Good. Southriver appreciates it."

Kiefer glanced at her. "I didn't do it for Southriver. Well, maybe some of it, but mostly it's for you."

"Me?"

Was that disappointment in his eyes that she might not believe him? "Yes, you."

Her pulse picked up speed. Did she dare hope?

"Where have you been? I thought I'd never see you again."

"Around. I had a few things I needed to get straight in my head, then some things that I needed to do," he said almost too casually.

"I understand."

He chuckled. "I don't think you do. But I hope you will. Why don't you follow me?"

"Where?"

"Just trust me, why don't you?"

"Okay."

Sometime later Kiefer pulled through the gate of the old mill they had looked at during the block party and parked in front of the doors. What were they doing here? He waited for her to join him.

"Why're we at the old mill?"

"For that view."

"How did you get permission to go in?"

He directed her inside and then toward the industrial elevator. "Didn't have to. I own the place."

"How? Why?"

He grinned then pulled the door open to the elevator shaft and pushed up the wire door to the elevator car. "You're sure full of questions. But since you asked, I sold my apartment downtown. And bought this so I would have a place to live."

"You did what?"

He closed the doors, pushed a button and they started moving up. "It was time to give up my passion for living in the past and concentrate on the future. Since I was going to be working in Southriver, it made sense to live close by. It would be easier for being on call. I've kind of become attached to the community anyway."

"That does make sense."

"How like you to understand the practicality of decisions." The elevator stopped, he opened the doors and they stepped off. "Come this way."

They were in an enormous open space with windows along the entire wall facing the river. The orange and pink of the evening sun streamed through them. Lines were drawn out on the floor and work was already being done to build walls.

Kiefer took her hand and steered her toward a staircase at the far end of the space.

She pulled at her hand. "I want to look around."

"Later. We'll miss the sunset if we don't hurry."

Together they climbed the metal stairs. At the top they stood on a landing and Kiefer pushed a door open and let her go out ahead of him. They were on the roof.

"It's wonderful." From here Ashley could see where the river ran into the ocean. Birds swarmed then flew off above the marshland. The wind made the saw grass wave gently back and forth. It was amazing. Made more so by Kiefer being there with her.

Not far away were the chairs, footstools and table that had been sitting on Kiefer's balcony. A candle in a glass jar sat in the middle of the table.

"The only things I kept. Come sit." He took her elbow.

They both settled into their chairs.

"This is wonderful. I know you'll enjoy living here," Ashley said, as she watched the colors of the setting sun change over the water. Over the next few minutes they sat in silence as night crept in on them. Unable to stand it any longer, Ashley had to ask. "Why did you decide to continue your work at the clinic? And live here?"

Kiefer said quietly, "Because this has become my home. When you have a gun pointed at you it doesn't take long for you to realize what is important. You said very clearly and pointedly that I needed to move on and make some changes. This is my first step toward doing that."

"I'm glad for you. You deserve happiness."

"How're you doing post-Marko?"

"It was hard for me to accept that he would do something like that. I've learned a few things about myself too. You were right—I need to be more careful. I fought so hard against my parents but I understand them better now. I do think I've been working to relieve my guilt where Lizzy was concerned. I don't think I can ever give up being a crusader, as you call it, for the children in this community or trying to improve it, but I do realize that I need some balance in my life. I'm working on it."

"I'm sure you will. I have complete confidence in you. And don't give up being a crusader. The world needs more of your kind."

"Thank you. That was nice of you to say."

"Seems like we both have learned and accepted a few things in the last few weeks."

Ashley smiled. "What's the saying? 'You're never too old to learn something new'? You know this really is a magnificent view."

"You could enjoy it every day. There's plenty of room here."

"Does the second floor have the same view as this?" She glanced at him. What was he asking?

"As far as I know. But I was thinking more of you having the upper floor."

Hope soared in her. "But that should be yours."

"It isn't like you to be so dense. I want you to live with me. Actually, that isn't correct." Kiefer put his hand into his pocket and pulled something out then slid out of the chair to bend on one knee. He held out a ring. "I want you to marry me."

Ashley held her breath. She couldn't believe this was happening. Hadn't dared to hope for the possibility.

"Ashley Marsh, I love you. Will you be my wife and share all the sunsets with me for the rest of our lives?"

She just looked at him, speechless. Was this a dream?

A flicker of doubt went through Kiefer's eyes. This big, confident, intelligent man was unsure.

"What did you say?"

He shifted. "I asked you to marry me."

"No, before that."

He looked confused. "That I love you?"

"Yes. Could you say it again?"

He captured her gaze. All the sincerity of his heart was in his eyes. "I love you."

"That's better than any sunset I've ever seen. I love you too." She leaned down and kissed him. When they finally broke apart she said, "You know, you don't have to marry me. I know how you feel about marriage. That doesn't change how we feel about each other."

"Yes, I do. Because I want everyone to know you are mine. I know you would never betray me. You are faithful to those you care about. A commitment with you will last forever."

"I'll not fail you."

"Nor I you. So you will marry me?"

"There's just one more thing."

Kiefer sighed. "Heavens, woman, it takes a lot to get you to say yes. What else?"

"About you being overprotective…"

"I'm going to try—"

She put her hand over his mouth. "We'll work at a compromise, something we can both live with. I understand where you're coming from, and as part of my love I'll try very hard to not make you worry unduly."

"As part of my love I'll resist calling in the army when you are a minute late."

She chuckled. "I would appreciate that. Now, if you'll ask me that question again, I have an answer."

"Ashley, you will make me the happiest man alive if you will marry me. Will you?"

"Just try to stop me." She threw her arms around his neck and kissed him.

Two months later, Ashley stood in the doorway of the Tybee Island lighthouse. Her father reached out a hand to help her descend the steps. She lifted the long skirt of the flowing white wedding dress she'd fallen in love with the minute she'd seen it. She felt like a princess going to meet her prince. Kiefer certainly was hers.

Taking her father's hand, she stepped down and placed her arm in the crook of his. Kiefer was waiting for her along with all their friends and family. Much of the community of Southriver had been invited to the wedding. Because of her position on the council, the media were also present.

She didn't care. The only person who mattered was Kiefer.

They'd chosen to have a simple wedding. No attendants. Just them. She'd surprised Kiefer with deciding on the lighthouse as the venue and they had agreed on a dusk ceremony, knowing how much they both enjoyed sunsets. As she walked across the grass and around the corner of the building, thoughts of how far they had come and what they had overcome went through her mind. She'd almost lost Kiefer. She would never take him for granted.

The large white tent came into sight. Kiefer would be waiting at the end of the white aisle runner. The man who would protect her, the man who would stand beside her and the man who would let her cry in his arms when she was hurt.

She and her father paused before entering the tent. Kiefer stood tall and handsome in his dark suit. A smile formed on his lips and his gaze held hers. If she hadn't felt like a princess before, she did now. The love in his look was crystal clear.

Half an hour later she was Mrs. Kiefer Bradford.

The reception was every bit the party they had hoped for. Kiefer swung her around on the dance floor and Ashley giggled as he brought her close for a kiss. He couldn't seem to stop touching her and she had no complaints about that.

"I love you. Do you know that?"

"I do. And I love you. Thank you for giving me this." Meaning the wedding. Her happiness. Him.

"Hey, there, mind if I meet the bride?" A man who favored Kiefer stood beside him.

Kiefer let her go for the first time and enveloped the man in a bear hug then stepped back. "Jackson, my man, it's so good to see you. I'm glad you could make it."

"Wouldn't have missed it."

"Ashley, this is my cousin, Jackson Hilstead the Third." Kiefer put emphasis on the last word. "You know—the one from California—Aunt Georgina's son."

Ashley smiled at Jackson. "It's so nice to meet you. I'm glad you could be here. You're the one who missed out on the name Kiefer."

Jackson grinned. "Guilty as charged." He shifted and put a hand on a pretty woman's waist and brought her closer. "This is Charlotte Johnson."

"Hello, Charlotte, we're so glad to have you

here," Ashley said, as Kiefer and Jackson went into a deep discussion.

"You're a beautiful bride," Charlotte offered. "Gorgeous dress."

"Thank you. I think anyone must look beautiful when they're in love."

Ashley noticed the other woman glance at Kiefer's cousin. "I guess they are."

"Is there another wedding planned in the near future?"

The men turned back to them before Charlotte could answer. She clearly had it bad for Jackson. Ashley recognized that look because she'd seen it in the mirror since she'd met Kiefer.

The men joined them again.

"Ashley, I want you to make Kiefer bring you out for a visit sometime soon," Jackson said.

"We'll put it on our calendar. It sounds like fun," Ashley assured him.

Jackson glanced back. "I see Mother signaling to us. Better go see who else she wants us to meet."

Kiefer and Jackson exchanged a hug again.

"That's a woman in love," Ashley said as Jackson and Charlotte moved away.

Kiefer kissed her. "You think everyone should be in love today."

"That could be true but what I do know is that I love you."

"And I love you."

Ashley took his hand. "Want to go to the beach and watch the sunset with me?"

"Every day. For the rest of my life."

\* \* \* \* \*

*If you missed the first story in the*
SUMMER BRIDES *duet, look out for*

*WEDDING DATE WITH THE ARMY DOC*
*by Lynne Marshall*

*And if you enjoyed this story,*
*check out these other great reads from*
*Susan Carlisle*

*MARRIED FOR THE BOSS'S BABY*
*ONE NIGHT BEFORE CHRISTMAS*
*HIS BEST FRIEND'S BABY*
*THE DOCTOR'S REDEMPTION*

*All available now!*